ISSUES THAT CONCERN YOU

Cyberbullying

Tamara L. Roleff, *Book Editor*

GREENHAVEN PRESS
A part of Gale, Cengage Learning

GALE
CENGAGE Learning·

Detroit • New York • San Francisco • New Haven, Conn • Waterville, Maine • London

Elizabeth Des Chenes, *Managing Editor*

Articles in Greenhaven Press anthologies are often edited for length to meet page requirements. In addition, original titles of these works are changed to clearly present the main thesis and to explicitly indicate the author's opinion. Every effort is made to ensure that Greenhaven Press accurately reflects the original intent of the authors. Every effort has been made to trace the owners of copyrighted material.

Cover image © MBI/Alamy

LIBRARY OF CONGRESS CATALOGING-IN-PUBLICATION DATA

Cyberbullying / Tamara L. Roleff, book editor.
   p. cm. -- (Issues that concern you)
  Includes bibliographical references and index.
  ISBN 978-0-7377-5692-0 (hardcover)
  1. Cyberbullying. I. Roleff, Tamara L., 1959-
  HV6773.15.C92C934 2012
  302.34'302854678--dc23

                                        2011040126

Printed in the United States of America
1 2 3 4 5 6 7 16 15 14 13 12

CONTENTS

Tyler Clementi was an eighteen-year-old freshman at Rutgers University in New Jersey and a talented violinist in the school orchestra. Clementi was also gay—although not openly so. One night in late September 2010, Clementi asked his roommate, Dharun Ravi, for privacy. Ravi went into a friend's room next door and remotely started up the webcam in his and Tyler's room. Then Ravi and his friend watched and streamed live video of Clementi having intimate relations with another man in his dorm room. Clementi found out about it and complained to his resident assistant and other school officials. Two nights later, Clementi again asked for privacy in his dorm room, and once again Ravi streamed the video live over the Internet. The next day, without telling anyone of his despair, Clementi drove an hour to the George Washington Bridge in New York City and jumped to his death.

Gay Teen Suicides

Clementi is just one of several gay teens who have committed suicide after being cyberbullied. In fact, four other teens killed themselves within a month of Tyler Clementi's suicide after being cyberbullied because they were gay. Asher Brown, thirteen, of Houston, shot himself in the head after enduring constant harassment at school because of his small size, his religion, and for being perceived as gay. (On the morning of his death, he told his father he was, indeed, gay.) Billy Lucas, fifteen, of Greensburg, Indiana, hanged himself in his family's barn after being constantly bullied and harassed because his classmates thought he was gay. (Billy had never told anyone whether or not he was gay.) Seth Walsh, thirteen, of Tehachapi, California, hanged himself from a tree in his backyard after being tormented over a long period of time for being gay. Seth was found before he died and was taken to a hospital, where he lived on life support for ten days before he finally died. Raymond Chase, nineteen, an openly gay sophomore at Johnson and Wales College of Culinary Arts in Rhode Island, was the fourth teenager who killed himself within a month of Clementi's suicide. Chase hanged himself in his dorm room after being bullied for being gay.

A Cyberbullying Survey of Gay Teens

Researchers and social scientists claim that as more and more of the nation and the world becomes connected online, cyberbullying is increasing. According to a 2009 online survey on cyberbullying and gay youth, lead author Warren Blumenfeld says that one out of every two lesbian, gay, bisexual, and transgender (LGBT) youths (54 percent) are regular victims of cyberbullying. Blumenfeld's online survey found that 45 percent of the LGBT youth felt depressed, 38 percent were embarrassed by the cyberbullying, and 28 percent were anxious about going to school. More than one quarter of them had suicidal thoughts. "There's a saying that we've now changed to read, 'Sticks and stones can break my bones, but words can kill,'" Blumenfeld said in a press release about his study. "Especially at this age, this is a time when peer influences are paramount in a young person's life," he continued. "If one is ostracized and attacked, that can have devastating consequences—not only physically, but on their emotional health for the rest of their lives." The teens also believed that there was little they, their parents, or school officials could do to stop the bullying. Blumenfeld said, "They feared that there might be more retribution by 'tattling.'"[1]

Teens often do not think of the future; they may think that their lives are always going to be the way they are at the current time. If they are being cyberbullied because they are gay, many cannot imagine a life when all that will be behind them. To give them hope for a better future, openly gay advice columnist Dan Savage and his partner started the It Gets Better Project, in which people could upload videos telling how their life as a gay, lesbian, bisexual, or transgendered person has gotten better as they have gotten older. The videos feature ordinary gay and

In New Brunswick, New Jersey, Rutgers University students participate in a candlelight vigil for Tyler Clementi. Clementi committed suicide after being spied on and bullied on the Internet.

straight people as well as celebrities, and the message of the videos is one of hope and encouragement, that life does get better as an adult. Blogger and TV personality Perez Hilton says in his video, "I went through a point in my life where I was suicidal daily. . . . But you know what got me through that? Time."[2] Adrianne Curry says classmates called her a "worthless dyke" in high school, but adds, "These people were insignificant pricks. And I have never seen them since then."[3] As of June 2011, more than ten thousand videos had been uploaded to the site.

The Megan Meier Case

Gay teens are not the only ones who have killed themselves after being cyberbullied. In 2006 Megan Meier, thirteen, of Dardenne Prairie, Missouri, hanged herself in her bedroom closet after two days of being cyberbullied by a new MySpace friend. Megan's parents learned after her death that one of Megan's friends' mothers, Lori Drew, had posed as a sixteen-year-old boy named Josh, in order to become an online friend of Megan's. After the friendship developed, Drew, as Josh, began to post mean messages about Megan on Megan's MySpace account in retaliation for a falling out with Drew's daughter. Drew's final message to Megan, posing as Josh, read, "You are a bad person and everybody hates you. Have a [bad] rest of your life. The world would be a better place without you."[4] Megan's response was, "You're the kind of boy a girl would kill herself over."[5] Megan's mother found her nearly lifeless body hanging in her closet twenty minutes after Megan had sent her last message. Megan died in the hospital the next day.

Many people across the country were outraged when the Missouri attorney general declined to press charges against Lori Drew, saying there was no law against cyberbullying. (Drew was subsequently tried in federal court for crimes of computer fraud and was ultimately acquitted on all counts.) Since then, many local, state, and federal legislators have felt there is a need for laws prohibiting cyberbullying, cyberharassment, and cyberstalking. Others feel that current laws can cover cyberbullying and that there is no need for new laws.

The question of whether new laws are needed to prohibit cyberbullying is just one of the issues in *Issues That Concern You: Cyberbullying*. Authors in this anthology examine this and other issues related to cyberbullying. In addition, the volume contains several appendixes to help the reader understand and explore the topic further, including a bibliography and list of organizations to contact. The appendix titled "What You Should Know About Cyberbullying" offers facts about cyberbullying, and the appendix "What You Should Do About Cyberbullying" offers tips on what young people, parents, schools, and bystanders can do about cyberbullying. With all these features, *Issues That Concern You: Cyberbullying* provides an excellent resource for everyone interested in this timely topic.

Notes

1. Quoted in ISU News Index, "ISU Researchers Publish National Study on Cyberbullying of LGBT and Allied Youths," March 4, 2010. www.news.iastate.edu/news/2010/mar/cyberbullying.
2. Quoted in John Hudson, "Gay Teen Suicide Sparks Debate over Cyber Bullying," *Atlantic Wire*, October 1, 2010. www .theatlanticwire.com/national/2010/10/gay-teen-suicide -sparks-debate-over-cyber-bullying/22829.
3. Quoted in Hudson, "Gay Teen Suicide Sparks Debate."
4. Quoted in Richard Price, "How Cyber-bullies Drove My Daughter to Commit Suicide," *Daily Mail* (London), June 20, 2008. www.dailymail.co.uk/femail/article-1027554/How-cyber -bullies-drove-daughter-commit-suicide.html.
5. Quoted in Jennifer Steinhauer, "Woman Who Posed as Boy Testifies in Case That Ended in Suicide of 13-Year-Old," *New York Times*, November 20, 2008. www.nytimes .com/2008/11/21/us/21myspace.html.

ONE

Cyberbullying Is a Serious Problem

Ted Feinberg and Nicole Robey

> Ted Feinberg and Nicole Robey contend in the following viewpoint that cyberbullying is a problem that has become even more serious with the increased use of the Internet. Cyberbullying may be worse than traditional bullying, they say, because the bullies can remain anonymous and may do or say things that they would not do in person. Moreover, Feinberg and Robey maintain that victims of cyberbullying are less likely to tell someone of the abuse than are victims of traditional bullying. They conclude that cyberbullying can have serious negative effects on the victim's social, emotional, and academic life. Feinberg is the assistant executive director of the National Association of School Psychologists. Robey was a school psychology intern in North Carolina when she cowrote this viewpoint.

Cyberspace presents a serious challenge for adults who are concerned about the safety and well-being of adolescents. Approximately 93% of U.S. youths ages 12–17 use the Internet [in 2008], a significant increase from 2004. The number of teens with online profiles, including those on social networking sites, also has increased. Importantly, 38% of high school students make efforts to hide their online activities from their parents.

A Serious Problem

Cyberbullying has grown in concert with increased rates of Internet use. In 2006, national law enforcement leaders estimated that more than 13 million children and adolescents ages 6–17 were victims of cyberbullying. Survey data show that a significant number of youths report that they have been harassed online in the past year. Further, research indicates a direct relationship between the frequency of cyberbullying and negative psychosocial characteristics and behavioral problems.

The problem for schools has grown as well. Although bullying and relational aggression among students are longtime concerns, the elusive nature of cyberbullying compounds the difficulty of identifying harmful behavior and intervening to stop it. Principals across the country are struggling to determine their authority over actions that technically may occur outside of school but for which the effects on students in school are very real. Cyberbullying can undermine school climate, interfere with victims' school functioning, and put some students at risk for serious mental health and safety problems. Out of sight cannot be out of mind. School leaders cannot ignore cyberbullying but rather must understand its legal and psychological ramifications and work with staff members, students, and parents to stop it.

What Is Cyberbullying?

Cyberbullying involves sending or posting harmful or cruel text or images using the Internet (e.g., instant messaging, e-mails, chat rooms, and social networking sites) or other digital communication devices, such as cell phones. It can involve stalking, threats, harassment, impersonation, humiliation, trickery, and exclusion.

The boundaryless nature of cybercommunications means that students can experience bullying wherever they have access to their phones or a computer: at home, at a friend's house, during school, and even on the bus or at the mall. A 2006 study by the organization Fight Crime: Invest in Kids found that 45% of preteens and 30% of teens are cyberbullied while at school.

Cyberbullying involves using the Internet and/or cell phones to post harmful or cruel text or images.

To their credit, many schools have made good use of filtering software that helps prevent students from using school computers to bully others. But this does not mean that cyberbullying is not a part of the school context or does not negatively affect students' school experience, and it raises many questions about the scope and prerogative of school intervention. For instance, is it a school problem if a student bullies another student in a text message that was sent while physically off campus during lunch? Or if a student posts a cruel message about a classmate on Facebook after school but the victim doesn't learn about it until he or she hears other students talking in class? Discussing the nuances of such questions with relevant staff members and legal counsel is vital to addressing cyberbullying.

Cyberbullies and Victims

Cyberbullies and victims are as likely to be female as male and more likely to be older, rather than younger, adolescents. Some cyberbullies and victims are strangers, but most often they know each other. A study of adolescent girls found that the bully was a friend or someone they knew from school 68% of [the] time and someone from a chat room 28% of the time. Some cyberbullies remain anonymous or work in groups, making it difficult to identify the abuser.

Like traditional bullies, cyberbullies tend to have poorer relationships with their caregivers than [do] their peers. They are more likely than nonbullies to be targets of traditional bullying, to engage in delinquent behavior and frequent substance use, and to be daily Internet users.

Cyberbullies can have different goals. Some do not see themselves as bullies, but rather as vigilantes who are protecting a friend who is under attack. Others intend to exert power through fear. For victims who are normally considered weak physically or socially, cyberspace can offer power through anonymity or through greater skill in manipulating technology. Female cyberbullies often act in a group and may simply be bored or feel justified in their Internet attack of a weaker, less socially adept peer. Some cyberbullies do not intend to cause harm; they just respond without thinking about the consequences of their actions.

Approximately half of cyberbullying victims are also targets of traditional bullying. Victims generally are more unpopular, isolated, depressed, anxious, and fearful than their peers. Those at risk are more likely to be searching for acceptance and attention online, more vulnerable to manipulation, less attentive to Internet safety messages, less resilient in getting out of a difficult situation, less able or willing to rely on their parents for help, and less likely to report a dangerous online situation to an adult.

Consequences of Cyberbullying

Cyberbullying can cause significant emotional harm. Victims of face-to-face bullying often experience depression, anxiety, low self-esteem, physiological complaints, problems concentrating, school failure, and school avoidance. Targets of cyberbullying suffer equal if not greater psychological harm because the hurtful information can be transmitted broadly and instantaneously and can be difficult to eliminate. Aggressors can remain anonymous and are hard to stop. Not knowing who an aggressor is can cause adolescents to be hypervigilant in terms of surveying their social environment, both cyber and real, to avoid hurtful encounters. Cyberbullying also may be worse than face-to-face bullying because people feel shielded from the consequences of their actions and often do or say things online that they would not in person. In some cases, cyberbullying can lead to severe dysfunction, externalized violence, and suicide.

Some adolescents are more susceptible to instances and effects of cyberbullying than others. Adolescents who are socially well-adjusted and have healthy peer and family support systems are likely to have better decision making and coping skills. They are usually better equipped to ignore or effectively rebut cyberbullying and are less likely to escalate the situation through retaliation. Vulnerable adolescents tend to have few coping skills, poor relationships, mental health problems, and family difficulties. Some adolescents engage in or become victims of cyberbullying because of acute episodic emotional distress, such as from a romantic breakup.

What Schools Can Do

Research indicates that adolescents are not optimistic about being able to prevent cyberbullying. Victims of cyberbullying are significantly less likely to tell someone of the abuse than victims of traditional bullying, and when they do reach out, it is more often to friends than to adults. Adolescents can be reluctant to tell adults about the abuse because they are emotionally traumatized, think it is their fault, fear retribution by the bully, or worry that their online activities or cell phone use will be restricted. The most popular intervention strategy that is adopted by students is avoidance, such as blocking messages or changing their e-mail

Kids Stay Home to Avoid Bullying

Research shows that 160,000 students miss school each day out of fear of being bullied. Amost half of all young people are victims of cyberbullying each year—while only one in ten of them tell their parents.

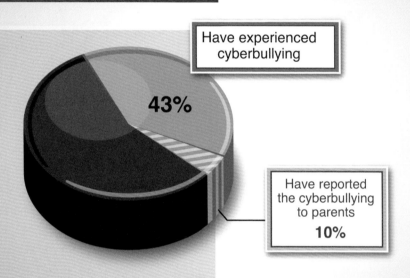

Have experienced cyberbullying

43%

Have reported the cyberbullying to parents
10%

Taken from: National Crime Prevention Council, "New Free Resources for Bullying Prevention," March 23, 2011.

addresses. This approach might help specific individuals, but it does little to change the overall behavior. . . .

Although cyberbullying does not necessarily begin at school, the behavior can have serious negative effects on the social, emotional, and academic functioning of the victim, as well as on the overall learning environment. Administrators must work with parents and community agencies to address the problem. Failing to do so sets the stage for potentially tragic outcomes.

TWO

The Problem of Bullying Has Been Exaggerated

Beverly Flaxington, as told to Michael F. Shaughnessy

Beverly Flaxington is the author of *Understanding Other People: The Five Secrets to Human Behavior*. In the following viewpoint, she is interviewed by Michael F. Shaughnessy of *Education News* and responds to some tough questions about bullying. Flaxington maintains that bullying is perceived to be a major problem mostly because of the intense media attention that is focused on it. According to Flaxington, bullying is no more prevalent or worse than it was a generation ago. She believes that the answer to bullying lies not just in legislation but in teaching children early on about the importance of self-esteem, better communication, and anger management.

[Michael F. Shaughnessy:] *Beverly, we seem to be hearing more and more about bullying and its various forms in the schools. How big a problem has this become?*

[Beverly Flaxington:] The problem has become bigger mostly because of the media hype surrounding it. We have had tragic cases, like Phoebe Prince right here in Massachusetts, where the issue of bullying has been connected to suicides but I do not think there are more bullies today than years ago. In fact, I can't find an adult who hasn't been bullied (and some very severely) at some point in their youth and yet when I talk to my own kids, their friends, my nieces and nephews (high school, middle school and grammar school) I cannot find one kid that says they have been bullied. We want to create "victims" and try to penalize the perpetrators but we haven't defined the scope of the problem yet. The one thing that I believe has changed is parental response to bullying. In the "old days" if you approached someone's parent, they might feel compelled to take action and work with their child. Today the problems I hear about are mostly with the parents and the attitude of the parents!

Different Forms of Bullying

Now, can you differentiate cyber bullying and in person physical bullying, versus emotional bullying?

Cyber bullying is at once [the] most benign but also [the] most invasive. It can be a nameless, faceless person lashing out at a child. The child has no idea where the issue comes from and can't understand [the] context or the source so it can feel much scarier, while at the same time, no one is there really threatening them. Physical bullying is easier to "prove" and so sometimes, while it may be the most physically painful, it is the easiest to address. If you hit someone, it's provable and you can confront them. Emotional bullying is probably the most destructive (and was at work in the Phoebe Prince case) because it is extremely hard to prove (my word versus your word); it is subtle yet very personal and we say things like "sticks and stones can break bones, but names can never hurt you." Unfortunately for many kids, it is the most hurtful of all. People who are being emotionally bullied will often suffer in silence because of the deep-rooted fear that they did something to bring about the reaction.

I am not sure what the school can do after 3:00 p.m. If a student is foolish enough to give out their cell number, do they not have any responsibility?

This is part of the problem—we aren't teaching kids how to manage themselves, we are just trying to protect them and make them feel as victims. Yes, we need to teach them awareness, consequences, safe behavior, etc., and in some ways if they make a mistake they do need to suffer some consequences so they can learn. Some of the worst bullies I've encountered have been bosses and co-workers of mine in my adult life so if we aren't getting at the root and teaching kids how to manage themselves effectively, and we are just seeking "punishment" for the perpetrators, we aren't doing our kids a favor. We aren't teaching them important life skills about how to manage themselves and make smart decisions.

In the schools, teachers cannot be everywhere, all day every day. But what should schools be doing?

What schools are not currently doing—teaching children how to communicate effectively, how to work through anger issues, how to connect with others, how to have effective "come-back" lines to someone who is picking on you, how to recognize a disturbed person versus an angry one—whilst also working to instill confidence in our kids and a strong sense of self-esteem. As one of my children likes to say, "Teachers have their jobs just because they want a place to get out *their* negative feelings. It's on all of us every day. Why can't they ever be nice and try to work with us to learn?" I think that sums it up pretty well!

What Should Schools Do About Bullies?

Beverly, there are school psychologists and diagnosticians who tell me that these bullies are seriously emotionally disturbed and should be in Special Education. Your thoughts?

This is part of the problem. We put all "bullies" into one group. One of the boys I know was called into the Principal's office for pulling a chair out from underneath another boy. They were trading off insults and he was the one caught. The Principal told him the next time something like this happened, he could be arrested and she tagged him as a "bully." This is very different bullying than someone who might be capable of violence! So, how can anyone say if we tag someone a "bully" they belong in a special program? I think part of the problem is our rush to define it, label everyone who exhibits the behavior and then punish them and put them away.

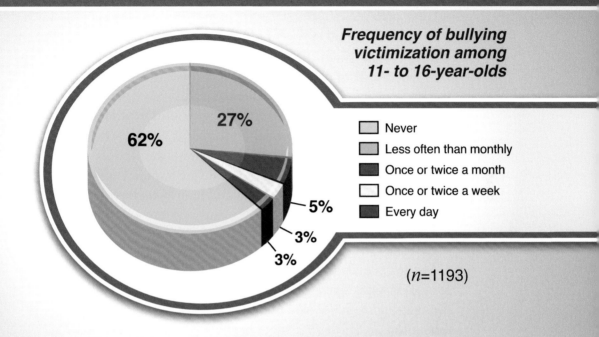

Frequency of bullying victimization among 11- to 16-year-olds

- 62%
- 27%
- 5%
- 3%
- 3%

Legend:
- Never
- Less often than monthly
- Once or twice a month
- Once or twice a week
- Every day

(*n*=1193)

Taken from: Michele Ybarra, Kimberly Mitchell, and Dorothy Espelage, "A Comparison of Bullying Online and Offline: Findings from a National Survey," American Educational Research Association, April 16, 2009.

On the same line, there are psychologists who diagnose these "bullies" as [having] "Conduct Disorder." Do you think this is appropriate?

Again, the same problem—we are trying to roll anything that might be negative behavior toward another child into one definition. We aren't trying to solve the real problem. Why are these children bullying? Why are our kids so susceptible to bullies? Why aren't we looking at each child individually? It's like saying that all crimes are equal. Is pulling out a chair from under someone a "conduct disorder" or is it an 11-year-old boy who thinks it's funny? We aren't digging down; we are just trying to diagnose, legislate and move on.

What about parents—should they not be held accountable or responsible?

Yes!! Parents are a lot of the problem. We need to be teaching our children healthy self-esteem, not "it's all about me" but how to have a solid core. A bully loses power if I don't give my power over to them. Parents need to work together and seek to understand the problems with their own children and try to work with them for a better conclusion. I believe parents hold much of the key but they aren't using it. Unfortunately most of us haven't been taught many of the skills we need, either, so imagine if instead of just legislating, parents and schools could work together to come up with some collective ideas about how to strengthen a child's self-esteem and help them have a Teflon coating toward a bully!

Elizabeth Scheibel, district attorney for Northampton, Massachusetts, speaks at a news conference about prosecuting students who bullied Phoebe Prince in person and online, eventually driving her to suicide.

When Does Teasing Become Bullying?

A lot of teasing goes on—but some would say it is a natural part of childhood to endure the taunts of their peers. Where does the line get drawn and who draws it?

This is another big part of the problem. We've started this rolling ball of "bullying" and we now look at everything a child does toward another child as "mean" and "bullying." If our children are in some sort of physical danger, we need to intervene and work with a child who is behaving in a threatening and dangerous manner, and with emotional bullying we need to call the children in and have a group discussion about how to solve the collective problem. Honestly, I was threatened more times than I care to remember that I would be "beat up at recess"—I spent much of 7th grade hiding under my desk, so should I have had these girls arrested instead? They are some of my closest friends now in adulthood. Today, there is a small minority of troubled children out there and we are taking the brush and painting every child who acts out as having a problem. I think it is scary that we aren't taking this one child at a time.

When should there be police involvement?

[When there's] violence, including weapons of some sort or a threat such as "I will kill your family" or "I will bomb the school to get back at you." The extreme cases.

I am not sure that making more laws in Washington [DC] is the answer—Who will enforce these laws? Principals who are already overwhelmed with AYP [adequate yearly progress assessments]?

Laws are *not* the answer. You cannot legislate emotions, feelings and most behavior, much as the government would like to. We need to have the school incorporating more proactive training, communication, and facilitation on this subject. We are so obsessed with "No Child Left Behind" and everyone's test scores that we have lost sight of the ability to teach children about the life skills they need that will serve them for the long term.

The Role of Guidance Counselors

What is the role of the school guidance counselor? Should they be on the lookout for bullies?

Yes, but I believe their role should be to work directly *with* the bullies. Instead of the boy who pulled the chair out being told he would be arrested and was a "bully" (which is a label that makes working with someone much more unproductive) what if the guidance counselor asked him, "Why are you pulling the chair from under Todd? What's going on?" What if our counselors actually used their skills to work directly with the bullies and help them to understand their own behavior? Again, imagine that instead we might actually teach them some life skills.

Are there warning signs that some emotionally disturbed child may begin to taunt and then physically attack others?

Children who are known to have been abused, children who abuse animals or talk about abusing animals or other children. Many times a child who is extremely withdrawn and sullen or exceptionally angry and acting out. But again, I've seen very disturbed children who wouldn't hurt a fly, and others who seemed "nice" [who have] been found guilty of doing terrible things to another child!!

What have I neglected to ask?

Your questions are excellent. Maybe ask "Is bullying the real problem?" I don't believe it is—I think we are living in a culture of blame and accusations. We like to label and judge others and we want to fix everything by legislation. If we could just turn our attention toward teaching our children life skills such as getting along, working through issues, strong communication, teamwork, problem-solving, organizational skills, presenting our ideas with confidence, etc., we would be developing mentally healthy adults for the future while at the same time minimizing the impact of the "bully" approach. If the school curriculum could be extended to give the children the opportunity to learn these skills, and work with the parents in the process, we'd see such a different outcome in the relationships these children are having with one another. It's sad—a missed opportunity for long-term positive gain.

THREE

Bullying Is Not a Rite of Passage for Youth

Michelle Obama and Barack Obama

> Barack Obama is the forty-fourth president and Michelle Obama the First Lady of the United States. The following viewpoint is taken from remarks they made at a White House conference on bullying. Michelle Obama notes that because it is sometimes difficult for parents to know what is really going on with their children, they must make an effort to get involved. She added that when something is wrong, parents must step in and take action. Barack Obama asserts that bullying is neither a harmless rite of passage nor simply a part of growing up. Bullying can have destructive consequences, and so, he maintains, parents, teachers, and students all need to work together to prevent bullying.

[Michelle Obama:] I want to thank all of you for joining us here today [March 10, 2011] to discuss an issue of great concern to me and to Barack, not just as President and as First Lady, but as a mom and a dad. And that is the problem of bullying in our schools and in our communities.

As parents, this issue really hits home for us. As parents, it breaks our hearts to think that any child feels afraid every day in the classroom, or on the playground, or even online. It breaks

Michelle Obama and Barack Obama, "Remarks by the President and First Lady at the White House Conference on Bullying Prevention," WhiteHouse.gov, March 10, 2011.

our hearts to think about any parent losing a child to bullying, or just wondering whether their kids will be safe when they leave for school in the morning.

And as parents, Barack and I also know that sometimes, maybe even a lot of the time, it's really hard for parents to know what's going on in our kids' lives. We don't always know, because they don't always tell us every little detail. We know that from Sasha. Sasha's response is—"What happened at school today?" "Nothing." That's it. It's like, well, we're taking you out of that school.

Parents Must Get Involved

So as parents, we know we need to make a real effort to be engaged in our children's lives, to listen to them and be there for them when they need us. We need to get involved in their schools and in their activities so that we know what they're up to, both in and out of the classroom. And when something is wrong, we need to speak up, and we need to take action.

That's just what Jacqui Knight did. She's a mom from Moore, Oklahoma, who's here with us today. We got a chance to spend some time with her before [the conference today]. But when her child was bullied, she got together with other parents and planned community meetings where parents and students could share their stories. They also held meetings for the public to raise awareness about bullying. And they've been meeting with the school board and superintendent to discuss steps that they can take to keep their kids safe.

Others Also Have a Responsibility

But parents aren't the only ones who have a responsibility. We all need to play a role—as teachers, coaches, as faith leaders, elected officials, and anyone who's involved in our children's lives. And that doesn't just mean working to change our kids' behavior and recognize and reward kids who are already doing the right thing. It means thinking about our own behavior as adults as well.

We all know that when we, as adults, treat others with compassion and respect, when we take the time to listen and give each other the benefit of the doubt in our own adult lives, that sets an example for our children. It sends a message to our kids about how they treat others.

So we all have a lot of work to do in this country on this issue. And I hope that all of you, and everyone who is watching online, will walk away from this day, from this conference, with new ideas and solutions that you can all take back to your own schools and your own communities. And I hope that all of us will step up and do our part to keep our kids safe, and to give them everything they need to learn and grow and fulfill their dreams.

At the White House in 2011, President Barack Obama and First Lady Michelle Obama (both at left rear) meet with students and parents at the Conference on Bullying Prevention. The Obamas believe that parents must become involved in solving bullying problems.

So with that, it is my pleasure to introduce this guy here—my husband and our president, President Barack Obama.

[Barack Obama:] Thank you. . . . Well, welcome to the White House. I want to thank Michelle for her introduction, and for marrying me—and for putting up with me.

An Important Issue

I want to reiterate what Michelle said. Preventing bullying isn't just important to us as President and First Lady; it's important for us as parents—something we care deeply about.

We're joined here by several members of Congress who've shown real leadership in taking up this cause. We've got a number of members of my administration with us today who are going to help us head up the efforts that come out of the White House on this issue. And I want to point out Judge Katherine O'Malley, the First Lady of Maryland. She is right here—Katherine. Thank you for being here. Thank you all for being here. You have a chance to make an enormous difference, and you already have.

Bullying isn't a problem that makes headlines every day. But every day it touches the lives of young people all across this country. I want to thank all of you for participating in this conference. But more importantly, I want to thank you for being part of what's a growing movement—led by young people themselves—to put a stop to bullying, whether it takes place in school or it's taking place online.

Bullying Is Not a Rite of Passage

And that's why we're here today. If there's one goal of this conference, it's to dispel the myth that bullying is just a harmless rite of passage or an inevitable part of growing up. It's not. Bullying can have destructive consequences for our young people. And it's not something we have to accept. As parents and students, as teachers and members of the community, we can take steps—all of us—to help prevent bullying and create a climate in our schools in which

Test Your Bullying Knowledge

How much do you really know? Check out these facts and myths about bullying.

Fact: People who bully have power over those they bully.

People who bully others usually pick on those who have less social power (peer status), psychological power (know how to harm others), or physical power (size, strength). However, some people who bully also have been bullied by others.

Fact: Spreading rumors is a form of bullying.

Spreading rumors, name-calling, excluding others, and embarrassing them are all forms of social bullying that can cause serious and lasting harm.

Myth: Only boys bully.

People think that physical bullying by boys is the most common form of bullying. However, verbal, social, and physical bullying happens among both boys and girls, especially as they grow older.

Myth: Bullying often resolves itself when you ignore it.

Bullying reflects an imbalance of power that happens again and again. Ignoring the bullying teaches students who bully that they can bully others without consequences. Adults and other students need to stand up for children who are bullied and to ensure they are protected and safe.

Myth: All children will outgrow bullying.

For some, bullying continues as they become older. Unless someone intervenes, the bullying will likely continue and, in some cases, grow into violence and other serious problems. Children who consistently bully others often continue their aggressive behavior through adolescence and into adulthood.

Myth: Reporting bullying will make the situation worse.

Research shows that children who report bullying to an adult are less likely to experience bullying in the future. Adults should encourage children to help keep their school safe and to tell an adult when they see bullying.

Myth: Teachers often intervene to stop bullying.

Adults often do not witness bullying despite their good intentions. Teachers intervene in only 14 percent of classroom bullying episodes and in 4 percent of bullying incidents that happen outside the classroom.

Myth: Nothing can be done at schools to reduce bullying.

School initiatives to prevent and stop bullying have reduced bullying by 15 to 50 percent. The most successful initiatives involve the entire school community of teachers, staff, parents, students, and community members.

Myth: Parents are usually aware that their children are bullying others.

Parents play a critical role in bullying prevention, but they often do not know if their children bully or are bullied by others. To help prevent bullying, parents need to talk with their children about what is happening at school and in the community.

Taken from: StopBullying.gov, "Test Your Bullying Knowledge," www.stopbullying.gov/topics/what_is_bullying/test_your_knowledge/index.html.

all of our children can feel safe; a climate in which they all can feel like they belong.

As adults, we all remember what it was like to see kids picked on in the hallways or in the schoolyard. And I have to say, with big ears and the name that I have, I wasn't immune. I didn't emerge unscathed. But because it's something that happens a lot, and it's something that's always been around, sometimes we've turned a blind eye to the problem. We've said, "Kids will be kids." And so sometimes we overlook the real damage that bullying can do, especially when young people face harassment day after day, week after week.

Frightening Statistics

So consider these statistics. A third of middle school and high school students have reported being bullied during the school year. Almost 3 million students have said they were pushed, shoved, tripped, even spit on. It's also more likely to affect kids that are seen as different, whether it's because of the color of their skin, the clothes they wear, the disability they may have, or [their] sexual orientation. And bullying has been shown to lead to absences and poor performance in the classroom. And that alone should give us pause, since no child should be afraid to go to school in this country.

A Series of Tragedies

Today, bullying doesn't even end at the school bell—it can follow our children from the hallways to their cell phones to their computer screens. And in recent months, a series of tragedies has drawn attention to just how devastating bullying can be. We have just been heartbroken by the stories of young people who endured harassment and ridicule day after day at school, and who ultimately took their own lives. These were kids brimming with promise— kids like Ty Field, kids like Carl Walker-Hoover—who should have felt nothing but excitement for the future. Instead, they felt like they had nowhere to turn, as if they had no escape from taunting and bullying that made school something they feared. I want to recognize Ty's mom and dad who are here today; Carl's mother and sister who are here today. They've shown incredible courage as advocates against bullying in memory of the sons and the brother that they've lost. And so we're so proud of them and we're grateful to them for being here today.

No family should have to go through what these families have gone through. No child should feel that alone. We've got to make sure our young people know that if they're in trouble, there are caring adults who can help and young adults that can help; that even if they're having a tough time, they're going to get through it, and there's a whole world full of possibility waiting for them. We also have to make sure we're doing everything we can so that no child is in that position in the first place. And this is a responsibility we all share—a responsibility we have to teach all children the Golden Rule: We should treat others the way we want to be treated.

Groups Are Taking Action

The good news is, people are stepping up and accepting responsibility. They're refusing to turn a blind eye to this problem. The PTA [Parent-Teacher Association] is launching a new campaign to get resources and information into the hands of parents. MTV is leading a new coalition to fight bullying online, and they're launching a series of ads to talk about the damage that's done when kids are bullied for the color of their skin or their religion or being gay or just being who they are. Others are leading their own efforts here today. And across the country, parents and students and teachers at the local level are taking action as well. They're fighting not only to change rules and policies, but also to create a stronger sense of community and respect in their schools.

Joining this conference today is a young man I just had a chance to meet, Brandon Greene from Rhode Island. Brandon is 14 years old. Back in 6th grade, when he was just a kid, he did a class project on bullying. Now, two years later, it's a school-wide organization with 80 members. They do monthly surveys in their school to track bullying rates. And what they realized is that stopping bullying isn't just about preventing bad behavior—it's also about working together and creating a positive atmosphere. So Brandon and his fellow committee members are now also doing activities like coat drives and community service at their school. And it's making a real difference. So we're very proud of Brandon and the great work he's doing.

Federal Efforts

There are stories like this all across the country, where young people and their schools have refused to accept the status quo. And I want you all to know that you have a partner in the White House. As the former head of Chicago's public schools, nobody understands this issue better than my Education Secretary, Arne Duncan. He's going to be working on it, along with our Health Secretary, Kathleen Sebelius. Arne is going to head up our administration's efforts, which began last year with a first-of-its-kind summit on bullying.

And we're also launching a new resource called stopbullying .gov, which has more information for parents and for teachers. And as part of our education reform efforts, we're encouraging schools to ask students themselves about school safety and how we can address bullying and other related problems—because, as every parent knows, sometimes the best way to find out what's happening with our kids is to ask, even if you have to—if it's in the case of Sasha, you have to keep on asking.

It's Hard to Be a Kid

Now, as adults, we can lose sight of how hard it can be sometimes to be a kid. And it's easy for us to forget what it was like to be teased or bullied. But it's also easy to forget the natural compassion and the sense of decency that our children display each and every day—when they're given a chance.

A couple [of] other young people that I just had a chance to meet—Sarah and Emily Buder, who are here from California.

They're right here next to the First Lady. And Sarah and Emily, they read a story about a girl named Olivia in a nearby town—this is a girl they didn't know—who had faced a lot of cruel taunting in school and online because she had had an epileptic seizure in class. So they decided to write Olivia a letter, and asked their friends to do the same.

They figured they'd send Olivia about 50 letters. But in the months that followed, thousands and thousands of letters poured in from every corner of the country—it really tapped into something. A lot of the letters were from young people, and they wanted to wish Olivia well, and let her know that somebody out there was talking—was thinking about her, and let her know that she wasn't alone. And because those children treated Olivia with that small measure of kindness, it helped Olivia see that there was light at the end of the tunnel.

Parents Must Guide Children

The fact is, sometimes kids are going to make mistakes, sometimes they're going to make bad decisions. That's part of growing up. But it's our job to be there for them, to guide them, and to ensure that they can grow up in an environment that not only encourages their talents and intelligence, but also their sense of empathy and their regard for one another.

And that's what ultimately this conference is all about. And that's why all the issues that we're talking about really matter. And that's how we're going to prevent bullying and create an environment where every single one of our children can thrive.

So thank you for the good work that you're already doing, and I'm sure you're going to come up with some terrific ideas during the course of this conference. Thank you very much.

FOUR

Cyberbullying Is Worse than Regular Bullying

Sarah Gibbard Cook

Sarah Gibbard Cook asserts in the following viewpoint that several teens have committed suicide because of cyberbullying. She cites expert Rosa Cintron, who claims that cyberbullying causes more anxiety and depression than traditional bullying because cyberbullying is often anonymous. Cyberbullying can also circulate to a wider audience in a very short time and can stay online forever, where anyone can find it, even if they were not looking for it. Cook holds a PhD in history from Harvard University and is a senior writer for *Women in Higher Education*.

Gossip isn't what is used to be. It has gone from over the fence to over the Internet, Dr. Rosa Cintron told student affairs professionals. . . . She's associate professor of educational research, technology and leadership at the University of Central Florida in Orlando. As lead editor of *College Student Death: Guidance for a Caring Campus* (2007), she was drawn into investigating "the awful experiences of campuses." Technology lets people do almost anything on a larger scale, including making students' lives miserable.

Sarah Gibbard Cook, "Gossip on Steroids: Cyber-bullying, Stalking, Harassing," *Women in Higher Education*, July 2010, pp. 18–19. Reprinted with permission from Women in Higher Education 2010.

Teen Suicides

Cyber-bullying has drawn national attention for its role in [the] suicides of several middle school and high school students.

- Megan Meier of Missouri hanged herself at age 13 after a former friend's mother took a male alias on MySpace, pretended to become her boyfriend and then publicly "dumped" her.
- Ryan Halligan took his own life at 13 in New Jersey after rumors spread online that he was gay.
- Phoebe Prince killed herself at 16 after months of face-to-face and online taunting at her Massachusetts high school. Nine teenagers involved were indicted on felony charges.
- Alexis Pilkington of New York got harassing posts on Facebook; even after her suicide, the nastiness continued on a memorial Web site set up by her friends.

Clemson University (SC) psychology professor Robin Kowalski found that cyber-bullying causes more depression and anxiety than traditional bullying, in part because it can be anonymous. With college students it's more often termed gossip or harassment but the effects are still devastating.

Why Humans Gossip

Gossip has always been with us. At its simplest, gossip is a conversation between two people about a third person who is not present. "Two-thirds of our conversation is gossip but only 5% is negative," Cintron said. Negative gossip is often about a conjecture that can injure another person's credibility and reputation.

Gossip long served a positive social purpose, law professor and privacy specialist Daniel J. Solove argued in *The Future of Reputation: Gossip, Rumor, and Privacy on the Internet* (2007). Public shaming enforced social norms by punishing violators. In most cases it was localized and short-lived.

In a campus study, Frank McAndrew, Emily Bell and Maria Garcia gave students scenarios and asked which gossip they would pass on and to whom. In their article "Who Do We Tell, and

© Dave Granlund and PoliticalCartoons.com.

Whom Do We Tell On?" (*Journal of Applied Social Psychology*, July 2007) they reported that damaging news about rivals and positive news about friends was most likely to be passed on.

For most of human history face-to-face gossip was a tool for negotiating and maintaining social status. Cintron compared its cultural role to the grooming ritual by primates and cats, which helps to hold relationships in place. Changes in society and culture have broadened the medium. They've also brought changes in the law, which is still in flux on the issue of Internet gossip.

Slander, Libel, and E-gossip

Slander and libel laws limit what can be said in print or on radio or television, especially if it's a falsehood about a private individual. Public disclosure of private facts may also be grounds for a lawsuit, except for celebrities. Insults written on bathroom walls are anonymous so it's hard to sue, but you can always paint over them.

E-gossip Is Different

Electronic gossip—via email, instant messaging, text or digital messages to cell phones, social networking sites, blogs, chat rooms or discussion groups—is different:

- It can circulate to a wide audience, no longer being limited in time or place. Even if the individual did violate social norms, the shaming is no longer in proportion to the offense. Internet gossip is out there for the whole world to see.
- It may stay online forever, unlike conventional gossip that eventually dies down. Once slurs are posted on the Internet it's very difficult to get them back down, and you can't just paint them over. Internet gossip is not so much like a scarlet letter as a permanent tattoo or brand.
- Like writing on bathroom walls but unlike word of mouth, it can be anonymous or posted under a fictitious name—and negative gossip usually is. Reasonable as it sounds to apply laws about slander and libel to harmful lies online, how do you know whom to hold responsible?
- Anybody can find the item by entering the person's name into a search engine, even if it's not the information they were looking for. If someone decides to post that your sister or daughter is "the biggest slut on campus," 10 years later that may be why she doesn't get called back for a second job interview.

"Once information is posted it becomes a permanent record," Cintron said. "Who will access it? What judgment will be made?"

Campus Gossip Websites

The rape of a Fordham University, NY, student was bad enough. Adding insult to injury, a few months later she found her ordeal being mocked on the now defunct Juicy Campus website, where messages said she deserved it. In another incident, Juicy Campus named a Yale sophomore, saying he had been in a pornographic movie and gave a link to a site showing him in explicit acts with men. About 900 viewers visited the site in just a few days.

Whereas blogs, chat rooms or social networking sites can be set up for legitimate purposes and then misused, the new campus gossip websites exist to spread malignant rumors posted anonymously. Anti-Semitism, anti-Asian sentiment and homophobia are rampant.

Innocent Entertainment or an Invasion of Privacy?

Site administrators say the sites are innocent entertainment, like celebrity gossip websites and tabloids. But celebrity status brings a recognized trade-off for privacy; being a college student does not. JuicyCampus.com, founded in 2007, listed by name the "sluttiest girls," the "biggest Cornell University cokeheads" or people with herpes.

Terms and conditions had users agree not to post anything "unlawful, threatening, abusive . . . or invasive of another's privacy." But invading personal privacy anonymously was the whole point of the site.

Juicy Campus gave rise to a firestorm of protest: on Facebook, in campus newspapers and in resolutions by student governments. At least two colleges blocked access and a few students brought lawsuits. Not surprisingly, the furor drew more attention and traffic to JuicyCampus.com. The site closed without apology in February 2009, citing low advertising revenues.

Remember *The Sorcerer's Apprentice*? Each time the apprentice breaks the broomstick, two new brooms take its place. Now there are Campus Gossip, enhanced with a section for photos and videos, and College ACB (for "Anonymous Confession Board"), with college-specific links and a redirect from the old Juicy Campus address.

What's a college to do?

Most student affairs professionals are familiar with Arthur Chickering's seven vectors of identity development, which shape the traditional-age college years. Among them are (2) managing emotions, (4) developing mature interpersonal relationships and (7) developing integrity.

Cyberbullying can cause more anxiety and depression than traditional bullying because it is usually anonymous and can be seen by large numbers of people on the Internet.

Because these vectors are still under development in college students, they are apt to exercise poor judgment about consequences, to themselves or to others. In emailing a nude photo to a boyfriend or putting a drunken video on You Tube, they rarely consider its potential to harm their reputations in the long run. Nor have some learned how to behave with integrity toward others.

Attorneys, courts and elected officials have not settled where to draw the line between free speech and harassment when it comes to the Internet. It's also unclear whether colleges can be held responsible in any way. In a recent case, a student's mother filed a civil rights complaint against Hofstra University (NY) for failure to act on her complaint about online sexual harassment under Title IX.

Universities Respond to Gossip Sites

How have universities reacted to gossip sites?

- Politely asked a site's leaders to tone it down.
- Called for a boycott.
- Hit the site where it hurts: financially.
- Spammed the site.
- Ignored it.

Fox Valley Technical College (WI) and Emmanuel College (MA) have spelled out policies for using Facebook. Antelope Valley College (CA) publishes guidelines for computer use and email, allowing campus action against inappropriate uses including "using electronic email to harass others."

While Americans once feared being watched by Big Brother, now it's their anonymous neighbors or classmates—armed with cameras in their cell phones—who pose a threat.

Soon a student may graduate into a world where there's no need to do a resume; potential employers will just Google her. No need to have interviews; they'll just look at her Facebook page.

Instead of enlarging our freedom, the Internet may reduce our freedom by taking away any personal privacy.

FIVE

Cyberbullying Should Be a Federal Crime

Lauren Barack

> Lauren Barack is a journalist living in Manhattan. In the
> following viewpoint, Barack discusses the recent testi-
> mony before Congress of students, educators, and parents
> urging the federal government to take action against per-
> petrators of cyberbullying. Representative Linda Sánchez
> of California recently proposed a bill named for a vic-
> tim of cyberbullying: the Megan Meier Cyberbullying
> Prevention Act. Sánchez contends that cyberbullying
> is hurtful behavior that can happen at any time and in
> any place and that victims of cyberbullying deserve pro-
> tection. She adds that laws criminalizing cyberbullying
> can be crafted to protect free speech while criminalizing
> speech that is intended to harm the victim.

Students, educators, and a parent whose son committed suicide after a year of bullying recently testified before Congress urg-ing the federal government to intervene.

"I think it's important to have zero tolerance against bully-ing," says Cassady Tetsworth, a 12th-grader and vice chair of the National Youth Advisory Board for the nonprofit Students Against Violence Everywhere (SAVE), testifying before House

Because laws already exist concerning bullying that is done in person, Congresswoman Linda Sánchez believes that laws should also be enacted against cyberbullying.

Subcommittees on Early Childhood, Elementary and Secondary Education and Healthy Families and Communities. "A federal law would make it more concrete, and not just something our school system wants us to do."

Federal Protection Against Cyberbullying?

Representative Linda Sánchez (D-Lakewood), who is passionate about this issue, agrees. She has sponsored the Safe Kids Agenda, several bills wending their way through Capitol Hill, including the [Safe Schools] Improvement Act—a bill that will require schools to launch antiharassment programs, and report any bullying.

But Sánchez, who spent years teaching in the public school system in Anaheim, CA, also wants federal funds available for schools to create antiharassment groups.

"Some schools in my district have a lot of gang violence," she says. "And many of the kids said they got involved because the gangs provided protection from being bullied and harassed. But when I spoke with many school superintendents to discuss the violence, less than half had any antiharassment policies in place."

Those programs might have helped Carl Walker-Hoover, an 11-year-old student who committed suicide in April [2009] after

State Laws Against Cyberbullying

States that have passed laws against cyberbullying

Taken from: National Conference of State Legislatures, "State Cyberstalking, Cyberharassment, and Cyberbullying Laws," January 26, 2011.

students taunted him for a year by calling him, "faggot," says his [mother] Sirdeaner Walker, who also testified last week.

Peer Influence

"It's important not to watch bullying happen and just be a bystander," says Tetsworth. "If you say, 'Hey that's not cool,' it sounds better coming from a peer. It's the power of positive peer influence."

But while that kind of group pressure works well in person, it does little when a student is faced with an anonymous bully online—whether that bully is a peer, or even an adult. An infamous case involves Lori Drew, a Missouri mother acquitted this month [July 2009] for her alleged role in the cyberbullying of her daughter's friend 13-year-old Megan Meier, who eventually committed suicide in 2006.

Bullying Must Have Consequences

That incident led Sánchez to propose another bill named for the teen, the Megan Meier Cyberbullying Prevention Act, which would set a prison term of two years for anyone using electronic means to bully.

"In older days, school yard bullies harassed kids for their lunch money, but children could still come home and feel safe," says Sánchez. "With cyberbullying it can come 24 hours a day, seven days a week and off school grounds."

SIX

Cyberbullying Should Not Be a Federal Crime

Louie Gohmert

The following viewpoint is a statement given by Louie Gohmert at a hearing on cyberbullying and other online safety issues for children. Gohmert asserts that children have been bullied as long as there have been children who are bigger and meaner than they are. He notes that laws designed to criminalize cyberbullying present significant concerns, such as encroaching on the right to free speech. True threats are not protected speech, he notes, and can therefore be prosecuted under existing laws. Moreover, Gohmert adds that if cyberbullying is made a crime, it should be under the purview of the states, not the federal government, since the federal government has no provisions for housing juvenile offenders. Gohmert is a US representative from Texas and a ranking member of the House Subcommittee on Crime, Terrorism, and Homeland Security.

As long as there have been children in this world, there have been bigger, meaner children who pick on them. As a small child, often the smallest in my class, youngest in my class in elementary school and junior high, I certainly know about that and about being picked on by bullies.

Louie Gohmert, "Cyberbullying and Other Online Safety Issues for Children," Hearing Before the Subcommittee on Crime, Terrorism, and Homeland Security of the Committee on the Judiciary, House of Representatives, September 30, 2009.

A New Kind of Bully

But when I was in school, the bully could be found in the lunchroom or the school yard, teasing kids, pushing others, or even taking things from them because they were big enough to do so. Times have changed. Now we have chat rooms, social networking sites, and use terms like "cyberbullying" and "cyberstalking." It appears the school bully has found a new playground.

According to the National Crime Prevention Council, cyberbullying affects nearly half of all American teenagers. Cyberbullies send mean text messages, broadcast insulting or degrading comments on the Internet, and even post pictures of the victim for others to see.

My own family has been bullied on the Internet by political bloggers trying to hurt me and my family because of my political positions. Liberal blogs have called me all kinds of names and made efforts to harass me. Some letters to the editor intended to intimidate and harass have been sent by e-mail. So perhaps this would be a way of stopping that.

Cyberbullying Tragedies

But 13-year-old Megan Meier, we know her tragic case in which she committed suicide after being told by a boy she had been talking to on MySpace that the world would be a better place without her. As we know, the boy, "Josh," was really the mother of one of Megan's classmates seeking retribution against Megan for allegedly spreading rumors about the woman's daughter.

Ryan Patrick Halligan, also 13, committed suicide after receiving taunting and insulting messages from his middle school classmates questioning his sexuality.

These tragedies are symptomatic of a much larger problem. Why do our teenagers and even their parents think this is acceptable behavior? What are we teaching our young people in our homes and schools about treating others with respect, as you would want to be treated?

Today we will be examining two bills that seek to address this new issue of cyber harassment. In the first, H.R. 1966, it proposes

Congressman Louie Gohmert, this viewpoint's author, argues that bullying is a fact of life and that children have been bullied for centuries. He believes that anticyberbullying laws would restrict the right of free speech.

a new Federal criminal offense for cyberbullying. Under this law, a person could face up to 2 years in Federal prison for sending a communication intended to coerce, intimidate, harass, or cause substantial emotional distress to another person.

Significant Concerns

This proposal raises several significant concerns, not the least of which is its encroachment on protected speech. The Supreme Court has identified those categories of speech that fall outside the protections of the first amendment, including fighting words, obscenity, or what the court characterizes as, quote, "true threats," unquote.

True threats of bodily harm are not protected. They are already crimes. But statements intended to coerce, intimidate, harass, or cause substantial emotional distress, however unsavory, likely do not fall within the category of true threats.

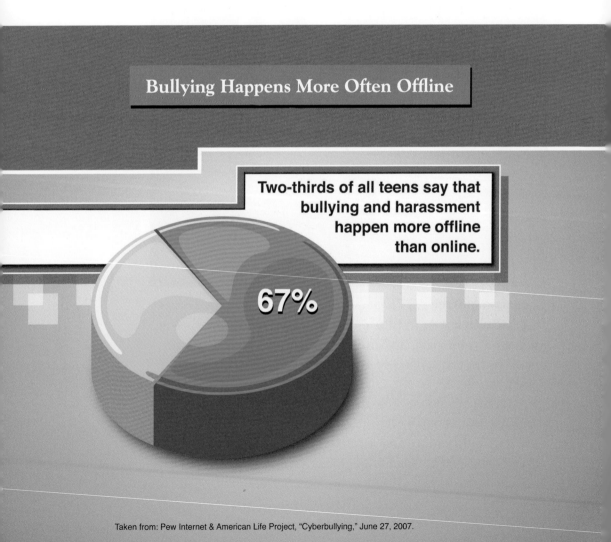

Bullying Happens More Often Offline

Two-thirds of all teens say that bullying and harassment happen more offline than online.

67%

Taken from: Pew Internet & American Life Project, "Cyberbullying," June 27, 2007.

Not a Federal Crime

Moreover, are Federal criminal penalties warranted for cyberbullying? Criminal law is or should be the purview of the States because the Federal Government lacks a general police power. As the Supreme Court noted back in 1903 in *Champion v. Ames*, "To hold that Congress has general police power would be to hold that it may accomplish objects not entrusted to the general government and to defeat the operation of the 10th amendment." And, according to the Congressional Research Service, 26 States have already enacted cyberbullying statutes, the majority of which carry misdemeanor, not felony, penalties.

Unlike cyberstalking crimes, which typically involve a credible threat of harm to the victim, cyberbullying does not. Cyberbullying is characterized as intending embarrassment, annoyance, or humiliation to the victim. This conduct is deplorable, but the question is whether or not it is criminal.

Most cyberbullies are teenagers or middle-school-age children. The legislation proposes sending these young people to Federal prison for embarrassing or humiliating a classmate. In fact, underage cyberbullies tried under this statute would most likely be adjudicated as juveniles and not tried as adults. And since there is no juvenile detention facility in the Federal system, these juveniles would be housed in State or private detention facilities, if at all.

Other Organizations Can Do It Better

The second bill before us today, H.R. 3630, creates a new grant program within the Justice Department to fund Internet crime awareness and cybercrime prevention programs. But I have to question whether a new grant program is what we really need. A number of organizations with expertise in this area already operate Web sites to combat cyberbullying. The tips and tools offered by these sites are free to parents, teachers, and teens.

H.R. 3630 requires the Justice Department to first undertake a study on the nature, prevalence, and quality of Internet crime awareness and cybercrime prevention programs. Then the

Department must consult with education groups, Internet crime awareness, and cybercrime prevention groups and prepare detailed guidance for the grant program. This seems like a burdensome task, when we already have in place guidance from organizations like the National Crime Prevention Council and others.

The question is whether we need to spend another $125 million of Chinese money that we will have to borrow in order to insert the Federal bureaucracy into a problem whose true resolution begins at home. Congress should not try to replace the parent or the teacher.

We are currently involved in a truly bipartisan effort that includes efforts by the ACLU [American Civil Liberties Union], with the Heritage Foundation and [Subcommittee] Chairman [Robert "Bobby"] Scott and I, attempting to begin dismantling the vast overcriminalization under Federal law of between 4,000 and 5,000 Federal crimes.

Who Is the Bully?

Consider this: The playground still has bullies. When a bully beats up a smaller student and the smaller student goes home, gets on the Internet and says the playground bully is mean, ugly, and stupid, it is the smaller student victim that has now probably committed a Federal felony under this proposed law.

In our desire to address the problems of the day, Congress all too often legislates without first getting to the bottom about any unintended consequences and potential damages to the Constitution.

What happened to Megan Meier and Ryan Halligan is tragic, is devastating. But Federal legislation does not seem to be the answer. Responsible parenting would be a good answer. Accountability for our actions is the answer. Arming young people with confidence and sense of self-worth to ignore the school Internet bully may be the answer.

SEVEN

Criminalizing Cyberbullying Would Be Ineffective

Larry Downes

> Larry Downes argues in the following viewpoint that criminalizing online impersonations in order to stop cyberbullying creates potential problems and unintended consequences. In attempting to keep up with technological advances, the laws can be both too vague and too specific concerning behavior they are trying to prevent. As a result, they often do not address the cyberbullying behavior they intend to deter. Much of the behavior that is included in cyberbullying laws is already a crime. According to Downes, to criminalize online behavior that is not a crime if it is done face-to-face does not make sense and would most likely be unconstitutional. Downes is an author and consultant on the law and the digital age.

I was interviewed yesterday [June 10, 2010] for the local Fox [Network] affiliate on [proposed California state law] Cal. SB 1411, which criminalizes online impersonations (or "e-personation") under certain circumstances.

On paper, of course, this sounds like a fine idea. As Palo Alto State Senator Joe Simitian, the bill's sponsor, put it, "The Internet makes many things easier. One of those, unfortunately, is pretending

Larry Downes, "The Fallacy of e-personation Laws," LarryDowns.com (blog), June 11, 2010. www.larrydownes.com. Copyright © 2010 by Larry Downes. All rights reserved. Reproduced by permission.

to be someone else. When that happens with the intent of causing harm, folks need a law they can turn to."

Or do they?

The Problem with New Laws for New Technology

SB 1411 would make a great exam question or short paper assignment for an information law course. It's short, is loaded with good intentions, and on first blush looks perfectly reasonable—just extending existing harassment, intimidation and fraud laws to the modern context of online activity. Unfortunately, a care-

Cyberbullying: What the Research Tells Us

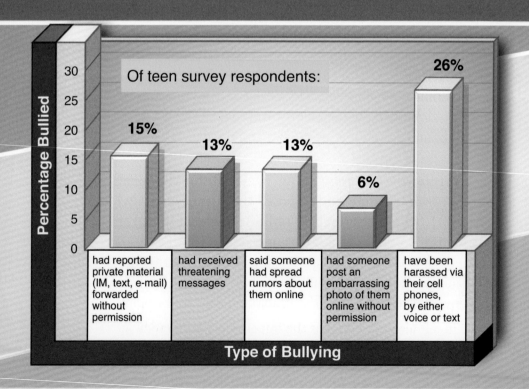

Of teen survey respondents:

Type of Bullying	Percentage Bullied
had reported private material (IM, text, e-mail) forwarded without permission	15%
had received threatening messages	13%
said someone had spread rumors about them online	13%
had someone post an embarrassing photo of them online without permission	6%
have been harassed via their cell phones, by either voice or text	26%

Taken from: Pew Internet & American Life Project, "Cyberbullying," June 27, 2007, and "Teens and Mobile Phones," April 20, 2010.

ful read reveals all sorts of potential problems and unintended consequences.

A number of states have passed new laws in the wake of highly-publicized cyberstalking and bullying incidents, including the tragic case involving a young girl's suicide after being dumped by her online MySpace boyfriend, who turned out to be a made-up character created for the purpose of hurting her feelings. . . .

Missouri passed a cyberbullying law when it turned out there was no federal law that covered the behavior in the MySpace case. Texas and New York recently enacted laws similar to SB 1411, though the Texas law applies only to impersonation on social media sites.

The problem with all these laws generally is that the authors aren't clear what behaviors exactly they are trying to criminalize. And, mindful of the fact that the evolution of digital life is happening much faster than any legislative body can hope to keep up with, these laws are often written to be both too specific (the technology changes) and too broad (the behavior is undefined). As a result, they often don't wind up covering the behavior they intend to deter, and, left on the books, can often come back to life when prosecutors need something to hang a case on that otherwise doesn't look illegal.

Given the proximity to free speech issues, the vagueness of many of these laws makes them good candidates for First Amendment challenges, and many have fallen on that sword.

California's SB 1411 as a Case in Point

SB 1411, which passed in the State Senate, suffers from all of these defects. It punishes the impersonation of an "actual person through or on an Internet Web site or by other electronic means for purposes of harming, intimidating, threatening or defrauding another person." It requires the impersonator to knowingly commit the crime and do so without the consent of the person they are imitating. It also requires that the impersonation be credible. Punishment for violation can include a year in jail and a suit brought by the victim for punitive damages.

First let's consider a few hypotheticals, starting with the one that inspired the law, the MySpace case noted above. Since the boy whose profile lured the victim into an online romance that was then cruelly terminated was a made-up person (the perpetrators found some photo of a suitably shirtless teen and built a personality around it), SB 1411 would not apply had it been the law in Missouri. The boy was not an "actual person," and, except perhaps to a thirteen-year-old with existing mental health problems, may not have been credible either. (The determination of "credibility" under SB 1411 would presumably be based on the "reasonable person" standard.) Likewise, law enforcement agents creating fake Craigslist ads to smoke out drug buyers, child molesters, or customers of sex workers would also not be violating the law.

Many Impersonations Are Not Credible

Also excluded from SB 1411 would probably be those who use Craigslist to get back at exes or other people they are angry at by placing ads promising sex to anyone who stops by, and then gives the address of the person they are trying to get even with. In most cases, these ads are not credible impersonations of the victim; they are meant to offend them but not to convince a reasonable third person that they really speak for the victim. A fake Facebook page for a teacher who proceeds to make cruel or otherwise harmful statements about her students, likewise, would not be a credible impersonation.

The Twitter profiles being created to issue fake press releases purportedly on behalf of BP would also not be illegal under SB 1411. First, BP is not an "actual person." Second, Twitter profiles such as BPGlobalPR are clearly parodies—they are issuing statements they believe to be what BP would say if it were telling the truth about its actions in relation to the gulf [oil] spill [of April 2010]. ("We're on a seafood diet—When we see food, we eat it! Unless that food is seafood from the Gulf. Yuck to that.") Again, not a credible impersonation.

You also do not commit the crime by confusing people inadvertently. There are several people I am aware of online named Larry Downes, including a New Jersey state natural resources regulator, a radio station executive and conservative commentator, a cage fighter and a veterinarian who lives in a nearby community. (The latter is a distant cousin.) Facebook alone has 11 profiles with my name. Only one of them is actually me, but the others are not knowingly impersonating me just because they use the same name, even if some third person might be confused to my detriment.

Websites Are Not Liable
Likewise, the statute doesn't reach out to those who help the perpetrator, intentionally or otherwise. The "Internet Web sites" or providers of other electronic means aren't themselves subject to

Opponents of anticyberbullying laws contend that, by being too vague, such laws make it difficult to determine which cyberbullying behaviors can be prosecuted. Many also believe that social networking sites such as MySpace and Facebook should not be liable for bullying posts on their sites.

prosecution or civil cases brought by the victims of the impersonation. So Craigslist, MySpace, Facebook, and Twitter aren't liable here, nor are the ISPs [Internet service providers] of the perpetrators, even if made aware of the activity of their users and/or customers.

For one thing, a federal law, Section 230, immunizes providers against that kind of liability under most circumstances. Last week [early June 2010], Craigslist lost its bid to preclude a California lawsuit using Section 230 as its defense when sued by the victim of fake posts soliciting sex and offering to give away his possessions. The victim informed Craigslist of the problem, and the company promised to take action to stop future posts but did not succeed. But it lost its immunity only by promising to help which, of course, the site won't do in the future!

So there are important limitations (some added through recent amendments) to SB 1411 that reduce the possibility of its being applied to speech that is otherwise protected or immunized by federal law. (In the BP example, the company might have a trademark case to bring.) Most of these limits, however, seem to take any teeth out of the statute, and seem to exclude most of the behavior Sen. Simitian says he is concerned about.

Unintended Consequences

What's left? Imagine a case where, angry at you, I create a fake Facebook profile that purports to represent you. I post material there that is not so outrageous that the impersonation is no longer credible, but which still has the intent of harming, intimidating, threatening or defrauding you. Perhaps I report, pretending to be you, about all of my extravagant purchases (but not so extravagant that I am not credible), leading your friends to believe you are spending beyond your means. You find out, and find my actions intimidating or threatening.

Perhaps I announce that you have defaulted on your mortgage and are being foreclosed, leading your creditors to seek security on your other debts. Perhaps I threaten to continue posting stories of your sexual exploits, forcing you to pay me blackmail to save you embarrassment.

The Truth as a Defense

Would these cases be covered under SB 1411? Perhaps, unless of course the claims that I am making as you turn out to be true. In the U.S., truth is a defense to defamation, so even if my intent is to "harm" you by revealing these facts, if they are facts then there is no action for defamation. That I say the facts pretending to be you, under SB 1411, would appear to turn a protected activity into a crime, perhaps not what the drafters intended and perhaps not something that would stand up in court. (The truth-as-defense in defamation cases rests on First Amendment principles—you can't be prosecuted for saying the truth.)

Already a Crime

Of course, much of the other behavior I described above is already a crime in California—in particular, various forms of intimidation, harassment and, by definition, fraud. The authors of SB 1411 believe the new law is needed to extend those crimes to cover the use of "Internet Web sites" and "other electronic means," but there's no reason to believe that the technology used is any bar to prosecutions under existing law. (Indeed, the use of electronic communications to commit the acts would extend the possible criminal laws that apply, since electronic communications are generally considered interstate commerce and thus subject to federal as well as state laws.)

For the most part, then, SB 1411 covers very little new behavior, and little of the behavior its drafters thought needed to be criminalized. For an impersonation to be damaging would, in most cases, mean that it was also not credible. Pretending to be me and telling the truth could be harmful, but probably a form of protected speech. Pretending to be me in order to defraud a third party is already a crime—that is the crime of identity theft.

The Law Is Not Harmless

Which is not to say, pun intended, that the proposed law is harmless. For in addition to categories of behavior already covered by existing law, SB 1411 makes it a crime to impersonate someone with the purpose of "harming" "another person." There is, not surprisingly, no definition given for what it means to have the purpose of "harming," nor is it clear if "another person" refers only to the person whose identity has been usurped, or includes some third party (perhaps a family member or friend of that person, perhaps their employer.)

Having a purpose of "harming" "another person" is incredibly vague, and can cover a wide range of behaviors that wouldn't, in offline contexts, be subject to criminal prosecution. The only difference would be that the intended harm here would be operationalized through online channels, and would take the form of a credible impersonation of some actual person.

Unconstitutional

Why those differences ought to result in a year in jail doesn't make much sense. Consequently, an attempt to use the law to prosecute "harmful" behavior would be met with a strong constitutional objection.

That's my read of the bill, in any case. Since I posed this as an exam question, I'm offering extra credit for anyone who can come up with examples—there are none given by the California State Senate—of situations where the law would actually apply and that would not already be illegal and which would not be subject to plausible constitutional challenges.

EIGHT

Only Adults Who Bully Children Online Should Be Prosecuted

Berin Szoka

> The real problem with cyberbullying is not kids bullying other kids or adults being rude to each other online, argues Berin Szoka in the following viewpoint. It is the problem of adults deliberately harassing someone online whom they know is a child. This harassment can cause real harm, and criminal sanctions may be appropriate, he asserts. Szoka also maintains that the best approach to combat cyberbullying between children is through education and programs that raise awareness of the problem. Szoka is a senior fellow at and the director of the Center for Internet Freedom at the Progress and Freedom Foundation.

The House Judiciary Committee's Crime subcommittee held a hearing yesterday [September 30, 2009] on the painful issues of cyberbullying. Rep. Linda Sánchez (D-CA) talked about her bill, the "Megan Meier Cyber Bullying Prevention Act" (H.R. 1966), which would create a new federal felony to punish cyber-harassment, including fines and jail time for violators. Rep. Debbie Wasserman Schultz (D-FL) talked about her bill, the "Adolescent Web Awareness Requires Education Act (AWARE Act)" (H.R. 3630), which would instead allocate $125 million over five years in grants for education and awareness-building about these problems.

Without endorsing any particular approach, Adam [Thierer] and I discussed the general advantages of education over criminalization in our "Cyberbullying Legislation: Why Education Is Preferable to Regulation" paper published by PFF [the Progress and Freedom Foundation] in June [2009], which we updated and submitted as written testimony. But we really couldn't have done a better job at making this point than Ranking Member Louie Gohmert (R-TX), who powerfully articulated his opposition to the run-away growth of federal criminal law. Chairman [Robert "Bobby"] Scott (D-VA) also expressed a commendable reluctance to just pass another law and assume that fixes the problem.

Problems with Criminalization

Three lawyers on the panel generally agreed on the thorny speech and due process concerns raised by criminalization and agreed that the Sánchez bill would require serious revision to pass constitutional muster. UVA [University of Virginia] Law Prof. Robert O'Neil suggested that of the exceptions to free speech protection recognized by the Supreme Court, the only one that could likely be used to do what advocates of cyberbullying criminalization want to accomplish is the intentional infliction of emotional distress. But O'Neill emphasized that this is generally a *tort* [a wrongful act], not a *criminal action*—which seems like a pretty big distinction to me, especially when the criminal sanction might involve a *felony* conviction, as Sánchez has proposed. Felony convictions are the "Mark of Cain" in modern life, exceeded only in their lasting effect by being required to register on a sex offender registry. Cato [Institute] Adjunct Fellow and civil rights lawyer Harvey Silverglate highlighted the serious problems raised by vagueness and over-breadth in attempting to define harassment—as evidenced by speech codes at many universities. Harvard Law Prof. John Palfrey generally echoed these concerns.

Criminalizing what is mostly child-on-child behavior simply will not solve the age-old problem of kids mistreating each other, a problem that has traditionally been dealt with through

Types of Adult Bullies

There are several different types of adult bullies:

1. ***Narcissistic adult bully***: This type of adult bully is self-centered and does not feel empathy for others. Such bullies have little anxiety about consequences.

2. ***Impulsive adult bully***: Adult bullies in this category are more spontaneous and plan their bullying out less. Even if consequences are likely, this adult bully has a hard time restraining his or her behavior. In some cases this type of bullying may be unintentional.

3. ***Physical bully***: Adult bullying rarely turns to physical confrontation. In some cases the adult bully may not actually physically harm the victim but may use the threat of harm or physical domination.

4. ***Verbal adult bully***: Words can be quite damaging. Adult bullies who use this type of tactic may start rumors about the victim or use sarcastic or demeaning language to dominate or humiliate another person.

5. ***Secondary adult bully***: This is someone who does not initiate the bullying but joins in so that he or she does not actually become a victim down the road. Secondary bullies may feel bad about what they are doing but are more concerned about protecting themselves.

Taken from: Bullying Statistics, "Adult Bullying," 2009. www.bullyingstatistics.org/content/adult-bullying.html.

The fact that a US federal court overturned Lori Drew's conviction for cyberbullying is indicative of the difficulty in prosecuting adults for this offense. Drew's actions allegedly led thirteen-year-old Megan Meier to commit suicide.

counseling and rehabilitation at the local level. For all the talk of how to craft a criminal law (especially its definitions) to minimize constitutional problems, I was very surprised that no one at the hearing raised the critical issue of just *who* it is we're trying to protect and from *whom*.

As we emphasize in our paper, the real problem here is not cyber-*bullying* (kids bullying other kids online just as they do on the playground), or cyber-*harassment* in general (adults being rude to each other online), but the special case of *adults* harassing *kids*—and knowing they're doing it. That's not to say that bullying can't be severe or very hurtful, but it's best dealt with by parents, schools and mental health professionals (for both the bullied and the bullies). Given that what's at stake is free expression online, I just don't see any need to create new penalties to restrict conversations among adults: As the lawyers on the panel emphasized, the Supreme Court already recognizes exceptions to First Amendment coverage for "true threats," "fighting words," etc., which are already covered by state laws. But in certain cases where an *adult* egregiously harasses someone they *know* is a *child* over the Internet (what most people assume happened in the Megan Meier case [in which a 13-year-old Missouri girl hanged herself after being cyberbullied by a classmate's mother posing as a boy]), causing real harm, criminal sanctions might well be appropriate, but no one's yet drafted such a bill.

As Ranking [Subcommittee] Member Gohmert emphasized, even if such a law could be written to minimize First and Fourteenth Amendment concerns, a critical question of federalism would remain: Should the federal government assert control of an issue of criminal law that has traditionally been left to the states? This is not merely a constitutional question, but a practical one: The federal criminal justice system simply is not equipped to accommodate juvenile defendants. For this reason and because it is still unclear how to write a narrowly tailored law, if criminal sanctions are pursued as a solution, it may be preferable to defer to state experimentation with varying models at this time. Indeed, Rep. Gohmert may be correct that, under the Tenth Amendment, online harassment simply isn't the proper role of the federal government.

The Better Alternative: Promoting Education

Two child safety experts also testified, Judi Westberg Warren, President of Web Wise Kids, and Nancy Willard, Director of

The Center for Safe and Responsible Internet Use. Judi and Nancy both talked about the advantages of supporting education, but disagreed as to what kind of funding was really needed and who should award such grants. Nancy argued strongly that grant decisions should be made by the Department of Education, Department of Health & Human Services *and* the Department of Justice [DOJ] acting together, rather than by DOJ acting alone, as the AWARE Act proposes—lest we wind up with something like the "DARE" [Drug Abuse Resistance Education] campaign, which some educators think was counter-productive. Despite these differences, education and awareness-based approaches have a chance of effectively reducing truly harmful behavior, especially over the long haul. Such approaches would have the added benefit of avoiding constitutional pitfalls and subsequent court challenges.

The Siren Song of Intermediary Deputization

The real bombshell at the hearing was Prof. Palfrey's reiteration of the call he made in his 2008 book *Born Digital: Understanding the First Generation of Digital Natives* to restrict the immunity from tort law created by Section 230 of the Communications Decency Act as a way of addressing concerns about online child safety, including cyberbullying. Adam [Thierer] highlighted the problems with such an approach in his *Ars Technica* debate with Palfrey earlier this year and has highlighted the threat this poses to online anonymity for all Internet users. The basic premise behind Section 230 remains just as true today as it was in 1996: Holding online intermediaries liable for the speech or conduct of users of their sites or services would strongly discourage voluntary efforts to police online communities. Indeed, as social networking functionality has become ubiquitous online, Section 230 has grown *more* important as a "Cornerstone of Internet Freedom": Without it, online intermediaries would be forced to take sweeping steps that could massively chill online speech and threaten the viability of smaller site operators.

I was relieved that Palfrey got no questions about this issue from the Members during the hearing, but the buzz about the issue afterwards in the hearing room left me concerned that we're likely to hear more about this very dangerous, but understandably seductive idea in the near future. "Hard cases make bad law," as lawyers say, and I can all too easily imagine well-justified concerns about cyberbullying leading, with the best of intentions, to "Tort Reform for the Internet" of the worst kind—one that would do serious harm to the profound democratization of content and communications wrought by Web 2.0 tools.

NINE

New Laws Are Not Needed to Combat Cyberbullying

William Creeley

> In the following viewpoint, William Creeley argues
> that new laws proposed to prohibit cyberbullying at col-
> leges and universities are redundant. Harassment of any
> kind—and cyberbullying is certainly harassment, he
> notes—is already prohibited on campus. Furthermore,
> a court case has set a precedent for defining a consti-
> tutional harassment policy, and a proposed new law is
> too vague and subjective, he contends. What is need-
> ed, Creeley says, is enforcement of current laws, not
> new laws. Creeley is the director of legal and public
> advocacy for the Foundation for Individual Rights in
> Education.

Senator Frank Lautenberg (D-NJ) and Representative Rush Holt (D-NJ) reintroduced the Tyler Clementi[1] Higher Education Anti-Harassment Act in both the Senate and the House of Representatives [in March 2011]. The legislation was first introduced last November [2010], but failed to reach a vote before the end of the 111th Congress. . . .

---

1. Tyler Clementi was a Rutgers University student who committed suicide in September 2010 after his roommate secretly streamed video of him in a sexual encounter with another man.

According to Senator Lautenberg's press release, if enacted the legislation would:

> require colleges and universities that receive federal student aid to have in place a policy that prohibits harassment of students based on their actual or perceived race, color, national origin, sex, disability, sexual orientation, gender identity, or religion. Schools would have to distribute that policy to all students, along with information about the procedure to follow should an incident of harassment occur, and notify students of counseling, mental health, and other services available to victims or perpetrators of harassment. The legislation would require schools to recognize cyberbullying as a form of harassment and it would create a new grant program at the U.S. Department of Education to help colleges and universities establish programs to prevent harassment of students.

Unfortunately, based on this summary, it seems all but certain that the new bill recreates the significant First Amendment problems presented by its previous incarnation. . . .

Significant First Amendment Problems

Let's review these problems now.

Harassment is already prohibited on campus. Under Titles VI and IX of the Civil Rights Act of 1964, colleges and universities accepting federal funding are *already* required to maintain and enforce policies prohibiting precisely the kind of discriminatory harassment targeted by this legislation. Senator Lautenberg's press release claims that the bill would "require for the first time that colleges and universities have anti-harassment policies on the books," but this simply isn't true. Like colleges across the country, Rutgers had an anti-harassment policy on the books last fall, at the time of Tyler Clementi's tragic ordeal.

If Senator Lautenberg means that the bill requires schools to address harassment based on sexual orientation for the first time, well, that isn't true either. As Harvey Silverglate pointed out in his column for *Forbes*:

> What's more, courts have already held that discrimination on the basis of actual or perceived sexual orientation can count as gender-based harassment under Title IX, and that same-sex discrimination is just as prohibited as male-on-female or female-on-male discrimination. The Department of Education has agreed. As a result, this legislation is redundant, at best.

> Besides, if the bill's purpose is to explicitly prohibit peer-on-peer harassment based on sexual orientation, why not just amend existing law to do so?

Vague and Subjective Definitions

The legislation's definition of harassment is vague and subjective, and conflicts with Supreme Court precedent. If the new bill defines harassment anything like it did when introduced last fall, that's a big problem for free speech on campus because it replaces an exacting, clear, speech-protective definition of harassment with a vague and subjective one.

For the past 12 years, colleges and universities have been guided by the Supreme Court's decision in *Davis* v. *Monroe County Board of Education* (1999), in which the Court held that peer-on-peer hostile environment harassment was conduct "so severe, pervasive, and objectively offensive, and that so undermines and detracts from the victims' educational experience, that the victim-students are effectively denied equal access to an institution's resources and opportunities." This is a very precise definition of harassment, and it allows for an appropriate balance between protected speech and unprotected harassment.

Compare that definition of harassment with the one contained in last fall's bill, which defines harassment as "acts of verbal, nonverbal, or physical aggression, intimidation, or hostility" that are "sufficiently severe, persistent, or pervasive so as to limit a student's ability to participate in or benefit from a program or activ-

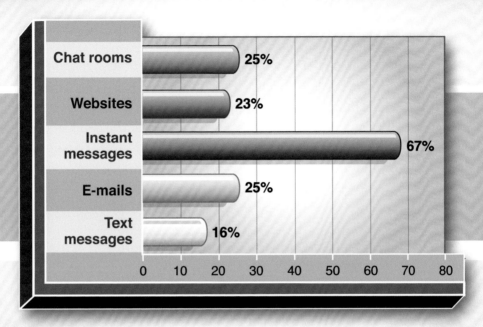

Chat rooms	25%
Websites	23%
Instant messages	67%
E-mails	25%
Text messages	16%

0   10   20   30   40   50   60   70   80

Note: Categories are not mutually exclusive.

Taken from: Centers for Disease Control and Prevention, "Electronic Media and Youth Violence: A CDC Issue Brief for Researchers," 2009. www.cdc.gov/violenceprevention/pdf/Electronic_Aggression_Researcher_Brief-a.pdf.

ity at an institution of higher education, or to create a hostile or abusive educational environment."

That may look similar, but it's not. There's no requirement that the expression in question be "objectively offensive," meaning that the most sensitive student on campus will be the one to determine what speech is and is not protected. There's no definition of a "hostile or abusive educational environment," meaning that college administrators will be the ones to determine whether speech is sufficiently "abusive" or "hostile" to warrant punishment. Unfortunately, . . . administrators will inevitably use this power to silence speech they find disagreeable, offensive, inconvenient, or otherwise, without regard to whether or not it's protected.

A Precedent Has Been Set

Making the bill's problems still worse, courts have relied on the *Davis* standard for years in determining whether or not college harassment policies pass constitutional muster. For a recent example, in *DeJohn v. Temple University* (2008), the United States Court of Appeals for the Third Circuit struck down Temple's former sexual harassment policy on First Amendment grounds because it failed to track the *Davis* standard. The Third Circuit held that "[a]bsent any requirement akin to a showing of severity or pervasiveness—that is, a requirement that the conduct objectively and subjectively creates a hostile environment or substantially interferes with an individual's work—the policy provides no shelter for core protected speech." Citing *DeJohn*, the Third Circuit echoed these same points last year in *McCauley* v. *University of the*

Critics of Senator Frank Lautenberg's (pictured) Tyler Clementi Higher Education Anti-harassment Act say many of the provisions in the bill are already covered by existing laws.

Virgin Islands (2010), in finding that the University of the Virgin Islands' speech codes similarly restricted protected speech.

Ironically, because the Third Circuit's jurisdiction includes New Jersey, any college in Senator Lautenberg's and Representative Holt's home state that maintains the definition of harassment proposed by the legislation would be in direct conflict with not only Supreme Court precedent, but also that of the Third Circuit—both of which are legally binding on public institutions in the state.

New Laws Are Unnecessary

New laws aren't needed to address "cyberbullying." Senator Lautenberg's press release states that under the legislation, colleges and universities would be required to "recognize cyberbullying as a form of harassment." While outlawing "cyberbullying" may make for a good soundbite on the evening news, the legislation ignores the fact that the behavior we're apparently now calling "cyberbullying" is already prohibited by colleges and universities across the country; it's just referred to as discriminatory harassment, intimidation, true threats, or other behavior that is unprotected or illegal. At the risk of sounding redundant myself, the abhorrent treatment of Tyler Clementi was *already prohibited* under both Rutgers policy *and* state law. The answer to the problem isn't new legislation; it's enforcing what we already have in place.

Young adults don't need special laws that treat them like children. It is strange to think, as this bill implies, that people who turn 18 and go to college are actually *less* able to handle one another's expression than young adults who don't attend college and instead head straight to the "real world." The idea of treating college students like children who need a mom or dad to tell them how to behave—the doctrine of *in loco parentis* [wherein the government or other organization acts "in place of the parents"]—went out in the 1960s. While other high school graduates and high school dropouts have to follow no more than existing law when they leave work and go to the park or go home to eat and sleep, under this bill college students—particularly residential students—will be treated like children who need special additional rules 24 hours a day, both on and off campus.

Education Can Help Prevent Cyberbullying

Debbie Wasserman Schultz

> In the following viewpoint, Debbie Wasserman Schultz contends that many young people do not realize the devastating consequences of their online behavior, including sending nude photos of themselves or humiliating a classmate. She believes that teens must be taught Internet safety and awareness of cybercrimes. Schultz asserts that education is important because it teaches parents and their children how to act in real-life situations, as well as teaching them to treat each other the same online as they would in person. Schultz is a US congresswoman from Florida.

You know, . . . as proud as I am to represent south Florida in the House of Representatives, the job closest to my heart is being a mother to my 10-year-old twins and my 6-year-old daughter. And, as one of only a handful of mothers with young children in Congress . . . I can assure you that we have no higher priority than keeping our children safe from harm.

Now, for me, I approach today's [September 30, 2009] topic as a Web-savvy mom with Web-savvy kids. In fact, as of yesterday, literally, my 6-year-old daughter now has an e-mail address

Debbie Wasserman Schultz, "Cyberbullying and Other Online Safety Issues for Children," Hearing Before the Subcommittee on Crime, Terrorism, and Homeland Security of the Committee on the Judiciary, House of Representatives, September 30, 2009.

which she uses on her iPod Touch—with strong parental control software fully engaged, I might add. Clearly, parents and teachers already know that our children are growing up in a completely different world than we did. . . .

Congresswoman Debbie Wasserman Schultz, the author of this viewpoint, believes that educating teens about Internet safety and cybercrime awareness is critical.

A Pathway to Risky Behavior

The Internet is a wonderful tool, but it has also become a pathway for risky behavior. The same Internet that helps our children create, study, and explore the world also enables minors to post nude photos online or text them to friends. The same Internet that allows children to organize clubs and volunteer for after-school activities also provides a way for children to harass their fellow students relentlessly, anonymously, publicly, and after the school day has long ended.

As legislators, we have to get real. We must accept that our kids spend more time online than in front of the television. We have to own up to the fact that 89 percent of teenagers have profiles on social networking sites like MySpace and Facebook. We must understand that nearly four in 10 kids have used the Internet to make fun of or post lies about their fellow students. We must understand that we live in an era when four out of five teenagers have cell phones, most of which have cameras. And we must know that more than one in five teenagers admit to sexting nude photos of themselves to peers.

These behaviors, often done on impulse or in boredom, have devastating real-life consequences. This May [2009], I had the honor of meeting Cynthia Logan, a young mother from Ohio. She told me her story, and it truly broke my heart.

Public Humiliation Results in Suicide

Her daughter, Jesse, was only 18 years old when she sent nude photos of herself to her boyfriend. After the young couple broke up, the ex-boyfriend sent them to other high school girls all over the school. They called Jesse names I can't repeat in this hearing. They passed around her pictures as casually as they would notes in a classroom. And they made Jesse's life a living hell. What began as a private communication turned into a public humiliation. Jesse became miserable and depressed. She eventually took her own life.

Sadly, her case is not unique. Megan Meier, the young teen from Missouri [who] is the namesake of Congresswoman [Linda]

Sánchez's legislation, also committed suicide after being bullied online. It is not surprising that researchers at the Yale School of Medicine have found significant links between bullying and suicide.

There are other dire consequences to these behaviors. An 18-year-old boy in my own home State of Florida was convicted on child pornography charges for sexted photos. He must now register as a sex offender for the rest of his life.

Tackling the Problem

So what do we do about it? There is no one answer or one silver bullet, but we can either continue to shut our eyes to the reality or we can tackle this problem head-on.

I believe that we must usher in a new era of Internet safety education and cybercrime awareness. We must teach children how to be good cyber citizens. Unfortunately, most parents and most teachers don't feel comfortable teaching kids how to be safe online. This means most children receive no training whatsoever in the safe, smart, and responsible use of the Internet. I, myself, have held three Internet safety town halls in my district. But as individuals and parents, we can't do this alone. We need a consistent and national approach.

The AWARE Act

Last week [in late September 2009], with [Texas] Congressman [John] Culberson, I was proud to introduce H.R. 3630, the "Adolescent Web Awareness Requires Education Act," or the "AWARE Act." Our bill will establish a competitive grant program so that nonprofit Internet safety organizations can work together with schools and communities to educate students, teachers, and parents about these online dangers.

Our bill authorizes up to $125 million over 5 years to establish age-appropriate, research-based programs that will encourage the safe, smart, and responsible use of the Internet and teach cybercrime awareness and digital literacy in the new media to our children.

Prevent Cyberbullying: What Schools Can Do

- **Educate students, teachers, and other staff members about cyberbullying**, its dangers, and what to do if someone is cyberbullied.

- **Discuss cyberbullying with students.** They may be knowledgeable about cyberbullying, and they may have good ideas about how to prevent and address it.

- **Be sure that your school's rules and policies address cyberbullying.**

- **Closely monitor students' use of computers at school.** Use filtering and tracking software on all computers, but don't rely solely on this software to screen out cyberbullying and other problematic online behavior.

Taken from: StopBullying.gov, www.stopbullying.gov/topics/cyberbullying/schools/index.html.

Education Is Important

Education is important because it helps teach both parents and children how to act in all kinds of real-life situations. Education is vital because it can reinforce new norms between students. Education gives children lessons, teaches skills, and builds strength that can last a lifetime.

We can teach children to treat their fellow students the same way online that they would in person. We can teach them not to bully or harass their peers and how to report dangerous or threatening activity when they see it. We can teach them not to post inappropriate material about themselves or others. We can teach them about privacy settings and about the risks of talking to strangers or posting personal information online. We can teach them that what they put online stays online. And we can teach them that the minute they hit that send button, they not only lose control over where their photos go next, they can also lose control of their future.

We can and we must teach children how to be safe on the Web. Jesse Logan's death was a tragedy, but it also is a powerful reminder about the lives that we can save. Knowledge truly is power, and with the "AWARE Act," it is my hope that we make knowledge our children's first line of defense.

ELEVEN

Schools and Parents Must Work Together to Stop Cyberbullying

Emily Bazelon

Bullying is not a new problem, asserts Emily Bazelon in the following viewpoint. Experts know that education and prevention programs help reduce bullying, but, the author says, it can be difficult to get the attention of students, their parents, teachers, and administrators to implement the prevention programs. School officials can talk with the cyberbully and with the parents to explain that such behavior hurts people and if taken further can be illegal. According to experts cited by Bazelon, schools should teach that cyberbullying is hurtful to all students, their parents, and the community. The best thing parents can do is to start a conversation with their children. Bazelon, a senior editor at *Slate* magazine, is also a senior research scholar in law at Yale University Law School.

Last September [2009], South Hadley High School in Western Massachusetts hosted a workshop on bullying for parents and anyone else interested. Attendance was low. As the school year progressed, a ninth-grader who'd recently arrived from Ireland, Phoebe Prince, got caught in a torrent of mean-girl taunting. In school, girls who didn't like the way she was talking to their boyfriends called her a slut. Someone scribbled Prince out of a student-body photo hanging in a classroom, one student said. Outside school, her tormenters ganged up on her on Facebook, making the bullying incessant.

In January [2010], Prince, who was 15, hanged herself. Both school officials and students connected her death to the bullying that preceded it, and the school committee meeting that followed her suicide was packed with 300 people. Many of them were parents, and some of them blamed the school. One father, whose daughter had also been bullied in ninth grade said, "This is not a new problem," according to the local paper.

Not a New Problem

That's why school administrators had convened the bullying workshop and asked anti-bullying expert Barbara Coloroso to talk to parents. The school had been looking at the problem of bullying for two years, they said, and had been about to convene a task force when Prince took her own life. They'd also been savvy enough to add warnings about online cruelty to the twice-yearly handout they give students about bullying, Coloroso said. Prince even got some counseling at school before her death, according to the principal. And yet none of this was enough. Prince's suicide stands as an awful illustration of how the Internet is making the old problem of fighting bullying even more difficult. It's not that prevention is a theoretical puzzle—the experts know a fair amount about what works. But actually implementing a prevention effort is another matter. It requires getting the attention of the whole school. And getting it before a tragedy, not after one, is no easy feat.

Difficult to Police

For starters, cyberbullying is trickier than the on-campus variety for schools to police. The basic conundrum is that harassment via Facebook, text messaging, and e-mail usually involves off-campus student speech, which is more protected by the First Amendment than what happens on school grounds. The standard is that schools can only discipline students for off-campus

Cyberbullying by Gender

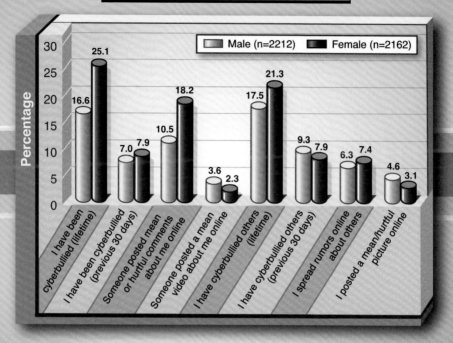

Note: Based on a random sample of 10- to 18-year-olds from a large school district in the southern United States.

Taken from: Sameer Hinduja and Justin W. Patchin, "Cyberbullying by Gender," Cyberbullying Research Center, February 2010. www.cyberbullying.us/research.php.

speech if it causes a "material and substantial disruption" within school. Online bullying that takes place off-campus is a new test for this standard, and courts are just beginning to sort it out. So far, they've been split. Some judges have said that speech that makes it difficult for one student to learn counts as a substantial disruption, as Nancy Willard of the Center for Safe and Responsible Internet Use explains. Other courts have erred on the side of protecting the First Amendment rights of students by ruling that schools can only discipline for bullying that disrupts school activities more widely. Unsure of their power to discipline, schools sometimes assume they can't do anything at all.

But that's never true says Elizabeth Englander, a psychology professor who directs the Massachusetts Aggression Reduction Center at Bridgewater State College. "They can always sit down with the cyberbully and with the parents and say: 'This isn't about discipline. It's about making sure you understand that if you take this further, you could break the law. And also you're really hurting people.' Often, in milder cases, kids underestimate how hurtful what they're doing is." Schools can support the kids who are targets of bullying, too, as South Hadley tried to do.

Bullying Prevention Programs

When working to prevent the new mix of bullying and cyberbullying, schools can look at the lessons learned from an earlier effort to stop the traditional, in-person kind of kid cruelty. After the rash of school shootings in the 1990s, a comprehensive study by the Secret Service of 37 such incidents found that many of the shooters were chronic victims of bullying who hadn't gotten help. Other research, conducted around that time, showed that bullying reduces school achievement. And so a series of prevention programs were launched at schools across the country. Some of them were shown to work. But this was before Facebook and text messaging became part of the bully's arsenal. So what translates?

The overall insight is pretty basic. "You have to work with the whole school—students, teachers, administrators, everyone," Englander says. "You need a new social norm, where the community looks down on these behaviors." How to pull this off? Essentially, a school or a school district has to decide to mount a public health campaign, like the ones that have reduced the rates of teen smoking or drunk driving. . . . To summarize the approach that the experts advocate: A school asks students how big a problem cyberbullying is and how, exactly, it's playing out. That assessment in hand, administrators and teachers start talking—to students, parents, and the community—about the damage it's causing, and they keep talking about it. They get parents' attention so they actually show up for workshops, for example, and absorb the importance of talking about the subject with their kids—the importance of taking the issue seriously.

Start a Conversation

The best thing parents can do, Englander says, is simply to start a conversation with their children. Ask teens and 'tweens where they go and what they do online. Ask if they've seen hurtful

Students (foreground) at a Pennsylvania elementary school wear shirts relating to the school's antibullying program. But, although education and prevention programs help reduce bullying, in many places student response to such programs is apathetic.

postings or texts. Ask what they'd do if they did. Schools can jump start this process by giving parents advice about how to respond, so they don't feel like they're fumbling around in a brave new world they don't understand.

If all of this sounds obvious, well, that's the upside. These efforts take awareness and effort and commitment on the part of schools and parents, but they're not technical or particularly difficult—you don't need to open a Twitter account to help your kid navigate the online world. That's a relief, because cyberbullying and traditional bullying are increasingly tangled up with each other. One 2008 paper found that about 60 percent of kids who said they'd been bullied online had also been bullied in person. . . . There are also, of course, kids who just get drawn in by the anonymity and ease of trashing someone online—just press "send" while you're at a safe remove from the person who's your target. But often the mean girls and the menacing guys online are the same ones who are mean and menacing at school.

What You Should Know About Cyberbullying

The Prevalence of Cyberbullying

According to a 2007 poll by the Pew Research Center:

- About one-third (32 percent) of all teenagers who use the Internet say they have been the victim of cyberbullying.
- One in six teens (15 percent) said they had had a private communication forwarded or publicly posted without their consent.
- Thirteen percent said someone had spread a rumor about them online.
- Six percent said someone had posted an embarrassing photo of them online without their permission.
- Girls are more likely to be cyberbullied (38 percent) than boys (26 percent).
- Older girls (aged fifteen to seventeen) are more likely to experience cyberbullying (41 percent) than any other age or gender group.
- Thirty-nine percent of teens who have Facebook or MySpace accounts have been cyberbullied, compared with 22 percent of those who do not have a social networking account.

StopBullying.gov, a government website that provides information about bullying, reports the following:

- Bullies are more likely to have criminal convictions and traffic citations as adults. In one study, 60 percent of boys who bullied others in middle school had a criminal conviction by age twenty-four.

- Fifty-six percent of students have witnessed some form of bullying at school.
- Most studies found that only 25 to 50 percent of bullied children talk to an adult about it.
- A 2005 study found that more than half of tweens say that if they see someone being bullied, they would say or do something to try to stop the bullying.

Cyberbullying and At-Risk Youth

According to the Gay, Lesbian, and Straight Education Network (GLSEN):

- A 2009 GLSEN study found nine out of ten lesbian, gay, bisexual, and transgendered (LGBT) students had been harassed at school during the past year.
- Fifty-four percent of the more than seven thousand middle school and high school LGBT students surveyed said they had been cyberbullied within the past three months.
- A 2002 study found that 78 percent of gay twelve- to seventeen-year-old students, or students who were perceived to be gay, were teased or bullied in school.
- More than four times as many LGBT students missed a day of school because they felt unsafe or uncomfortable (6.7 percent of all students compared with 30 percent of LGBT students).

Children with disabilities and special needs are at particular risk of being bullied by other children. According to the US Department of Health and Human Services, Health Resources and Services Administration:

- Children who stutter are more likely to be bullied than other children; 83 percent of adults who stuttered as children had been bullied as a child, and 71 percent said it had happened at least once a week.

- Researchers found in a 2004 study that girls aged eleven to sixteen and boys aged eleven to twelve who are overweight or obese were more likely than their normal-weight peers to be teased or bullied.
- The Americans with Disabilities Act of 1990 makes harassment of a person with disabilities illegal, and such harassment can include cyberbullying.

Cyberbullying and Sexting

According to a 2008 survey by the National Campaign to Prevent Teen and Unplanned Pregnancy and *Cosmogirl*:

- Overall, 20 percent of teens between the ages of thirteen and nineteen had sent or posted nude or seminude photos or videos of themselves.
- Seventy-one percent of teen girls and 67 percent of teen boys who had sent or posted sexually suggestive photos or messages said they had sent it to a boyfriend or girlfriend.
- Twenty-one percent of teen girls and 39 percent of teen boys say they have sent such a photo or message to someone they wanted to date or hook up with.
- Forty percent of teens (aged thirteen to nineteen) and young adults (aged twenty to twenty-six) say they have had a sexually suggestive message (originally meant to be private) shown to them.
- Twenty percent of teens and young adults say they have shared a private sexually suggestive message with someone else.
- Forty-two percent of teen girls and 38 percent of young adult women say "pressure from guys" is why they sent or posted sexually suggestive messages and images.
- Twenty-four percent of teen boys and 20 percent of young adult men say "pressure from friends" is why they sent or posted sexually suggestive messages and images.

What You Should Do About Cyberbullying

Many people consider bullying to be a rite of passage of childhood, something that many children experience, either as a bully or as the bully's victim. In the age of the Internet and cell phones, the opportunities for cyberbullying and harassment are even more available. Cyberbullies can post mean and hurtful remarks or photos on social media websites, send harassing text messages via cell phones to the victim, or forward messages or photos to friends with just the click of a button. The Internet also allows bullies to hide their identities—they can hide behind anonymous e-mail addresses and made-up screen names. Because the click of a button can instantly send the message, neighbors, friends, classmates, and coworkers can instantly read and follow a bully's cyberattack on the victim.

While some people may not realize how their remarks may be hurtful to someone, others deliberately use the Internet and technology to be malicious. Using the Internet to send nasty comments also allows a physically weaker person to turn the tables and bully someone bigger and stronger. Some feel it is easier to be mean to someone if they can hide behind written words and the remarks are not made face to face. In addition, because cyberbullying is so new, many adults do not yet know how to respond to cyberattacks or may not consider cyberbullying wrong or harmful. The Cyberbullying Research Center has developed a brochure to help students, parents, school administrators, and bystanders know what bullying is and what they can do to stop it.

What Is Cyberbullying?

According to StopCyberbullying.org's *Cyberbullying: Identification, Prevention, and Response* fact sheet, "'Cyberbullying' is when a child, preteen, or teen is tormented, threatened, harassed, humiliated, embarrassed or otherwise targeted by another child, preteen or teen using the Internet, interactive and digital technologies or mobile phones." Such harassment is considered cyberbullying only when it happens between two children or teenagers; if one of the participants is over age eighteen, then it is cyberharassment or cyberstalking.

Some examples of cyberbullying, according to the National Crime Prevention Council, include sending mean or cruel e-mails, text messages, or instant messages (IMs); posting these messages on someone's Facebook wall or other social media site; breaking into someone's account to send hurtful or false messages while posing as that person; creating websites that make fun of or are cruel to someone; using websites to rate classmates as ugliest or prettiest; and blocking someone's e-mail or IM for no reason.

Recognizing the Signs of Cyberbullying

StopCyberbullying.org gives the following examples of when someone may be a victim of cyberbullying: A child or teenager unexpectedly stops using his or her computer; is nervous or jumpy about receiving text messages, IMs, or e-mails; is angry or depressed after using the computer or cell phone; is reluctant or uneasy about going to school; avoids discussions about what he or she is doing on the computer or cell phone; quickly closes screens or programs if someone walks by; or becomes withdrawn from family and friends.

One or more of these signs may also indicate that a child or youth may be a cyberbully, such as avoiding discussions about what he or she is doing on the computer or quickly shutting down screens when someone walks by. Other signs that someone may be cyberbullying, according to the StopCyberbullying .org fact sheet, is if the child becomes "unusually upset if computer or cell phone privileges are restricted" or if he or she has multiple online accounts, especially if the account belongs to someone else.

What Youth Can Do

The most important thing a child or teenager can do to stop cyberbullying is to talk with a trusted adult, such as a parent, teacher, coach, guidance counselor, or minister about it. StopCyberbullying.org recommends that teens and children ignore, if possible, teasing and name-calling. Responding to minor attacks like this may encourage bullies to continue and often makes the cyberbullying attacks worse. In addition, the organization encourages victims of cyberbullying to keep track of cyberbullying incidents in a log or journal. The log should include the date, time, what happened, and what the victim's response was. Such a log can be useful when talking with adults about the cyberbullying.

In addition, everyone, not just teens, should go over their privacy settings on websites such as Facebook to block unwanted "friends" and to keep them from posting or reading messages on their walls or prevent them from contacting them via chat, IM, and e-mail.

What Parents Can Do

Parents should teach their children about what cyberbullying is and what is—and is not—appropriate online behavior. Parents should monitor their children's computer use and discuss privacy issues, such as what information is safe and suitable to post online and send electronically. Discussions should include the repercussions of what could happen if private photos and messages are posted or sent for anyone and everyone to see. Parents may want to draw up a contract or agreement concerning proper Internet and cell phone use, spelling out what is expected of the child and what the consequences are if the agreement is broken.

If a child is being cyberbullied, the parents should be supportive and do all they can to make sure the child is safe. Parents should talk to their child about what can be done to stop the cyberbullying, such as meeting with a teacher or school administrator, the bully's parents, or possibly with the Internet service provider or the cell phone company about removing the offensive message. If credible physical threats have been made or a crime has been committed, the parents should also contact the police.

If parents suspect that their child is a cyberbully, a discussion of a different type is in order. Parents should explain to their child how cyberbullying behavior can be hurtful to another child. The cyberbully should be made to face the consequences of his or her actions, such as having phone or Internet access taken away. If the behavior continues despite the parental warnings, then firmer and escalating penalties should be applied. Parents may also want to consider installing monitoring devices onto the computer or cell phone.

What Schools Can Do

Schools should have a written policy on bullying and cyberbullying, detailing what is unacceptable and inappropriate behavior. The policy should also spell out how the school will respond to both minor and severe cases of cyberbullying. For example, the Cyberbullying Research Center suggests that for milder forms of harassment, students be required to make posters or give presentations to classmates about cyberbullying. In addition, the center recommends that the parents be called and the victim and the bully be counseled about the behavior. The Cyberbullying Research Center emphasizes that schools must stress that cyberbullying "in any form is wrong and will not be tolerated." In more serious cases, such as those that involve threats against another student, detention, suspension, or expulsion may be required.

What Bystanders Should Do

People who witness bullying and cyberbullying know the behavior is wrong but often hesitate to step in to stop it. They may fear retaliation or the hassle of getting involved. Sameer Hinduja and Justin W. Patchin, who have studied and written extensively on cyberbullying, believe it is important for bystanders to do what they can to stop cyberbullying. They write, "We believe that bystanders can make a huge difference in improving the situation for cyberbullying victims, who often feel helpless and hopeless and need someone to come to the rescue." They urge bystanders to take notes about what they saw and when and where they saw it, and to then tell someone who can do something about the situation. Finally, and perhaps most importantly, they write that bystanders should never encourage the cyberbullying by laughing, forwarding messages or photos, or staying silent.

ORGANIZATIONS TO CONTACT

The editors have compiled the following list of organizations concerned with the issues presented in this book. The descriptions are derived from materials provided by the organizations. All have publications or information available for interested readers. The list was compiled on the date of publication of the present volume; the information provided here may change. Be aware that many organizations take several weeks or longer to respond to inquiries, so allow as much time as possible.

American Civil Liberties Union (ACLU)
125 Broad St., 18th Fl., New York, NY 10004
(212) 549-2500
website: www.aclu.org

The ACLU is a national organization that works to defend Americans' civil rights as guaranteed in the US Constitution. The organization publishes the semiannual newsletter *Civil Liberties Alert*. Its website includes congressional testimony and briefing papers, such as "Free Speech and Cyber-bullying."

American Psychological Association (APA)
750 First St. NE, Washington, DC 20002-4242
(202) 336-5500 • toll-free: (800) 374-2721
e-mail: public.affairs@apa.org • website: www.apa.org

The APA is the primary scientific and professional psychology organization in the United States. Its official position is that all forms of bullying exert short- and long-term harmful psychological effects on both bullies and their victims. Its available resources include the APA Resolution on Bullying Among Children and Youth. The association's website offers links to a research roundup, bullying prevention programs around the world, and a "Getting Help" section for adolescents and adults dealing with bullying issues.

American School Counselor Association (ASCA)
1101 King St., Ste. 625, Alexandria, VA 22314
(703) 683-2722 • toll-free: (800) 306-4722 • fax: (703) 683-1619
e-mail: asca@schoolcounselor.org
website: www.schoolcounselor.org

ASCA sponsors workshops such as Bullying and What to Do About It and publishes the bimonthly magazine ASCA *School Counselor*. Free online resources include the articles "The Buzz on Bullying" and "Appropriate Use of the Internet." The association's online bookstore offers titles aimed at young people, such as *Cool, Calm, and Confident: A Workbook to Help Kids Learn Assertiveness Skills*; antibullying posters, banners, and bulletin boards; and sample lesson plans for school-based antibullying programs.

Anti-Defamation League (ADL)
605 Third Ave., New York, NY 10158
e-mail: adlmedia@adl.org • website: www.adl.org/cyberbullying

The ADL fights anti-Semitism and all forms of bigotry in the United States and abroad through information, education, legislation, and advocacy. The organization serves as a resource on cyberbullying for the government, media, law enforcement, the public, and educators. It offers programs, interactive workshops, and advocacy for combating cyberbullying. Among the resources the ADL features on its website are "Responding to Cyberbullying: Tips," "Advice on Cyberbullying and Teens," and "ADL Recommendations to Federal Agencies for Federal Bullying Prevention Summit."

Center for Safe and Responsible Internet Use
474 W. Twenty-Ninth Ave., Eugene, OR 97405
(541) 556-1145
e-mail: nwillard@csriu.org• website: www.cyberbully.org

The Center for Safe and Responsible Internet Use was founded in 2002 by Nancy Willard, an authority on student Internet use management in schools and the author of *Cyberbullying* and Cyberthreats: Responding to the Challenge of Online Social Aggression, Threats, and Distress. In addition to briefs and guides for educators and parents, the center offers numerous reports, articles, and books for student researchers, including "Sexting and Youth," "Achieving a Rational Approach," "Why Age and Identity Verification Will Not Work," and the book Cyber-Safe Kids, Cyber-Savvy Teens.

Gay, Lesbian, and Straight Education Network (GLSEN)
90 Broad St., 2nd Fl., New York, NY 10004
(212) 727-0135 • fax: (212) 272-0254
e-mail: glsen@glsen.org • website: www.glsen.org

Founded in 1990, the GLSEN fosters a healthy, safe school environment where every student is respected regardless of sexual orientation. It is the oversight organization of more than four thousand school-based Gay-Straight Alliances and the sponsor of two antidiscrimination school events—the National Day of Silence and No Name-Calling Week. Its antibullying initiatives include the educational website ThinkB4YouSpeak.com and the monthly e-newsletter Respect Report. The GLSEN website offers research reports such as From Teasing to Torment: School Climate in America; A National Report on School Bullying and Shared Differences: The Experiences of Lesbian, Gay, Bixexual and Transgender Students of Color, as well as an antibullying toolkit called the New Safe Space Kit.

Make a Difference for Kids
People's Bank of Mt. Washington
PO Box 95, Mt. Washington, KY 40047
toll-free: (800) 273-8255

Make a Difference for Kids promotes awareness and prevention of cyberbullying and suicide through education. It was created in memory of Rachael Neblett and Kristin Settles, two Kentucky teens who committed suicide as a result of being cyberbullied. The organization runs a cyberbullying hotline and encourages kids in crisis to call.

National Center for Bullying Prevention
PACER Center, 8161 Normandale Blvd.
Bloomington, MN 55437
toll-free: (888) 248-0822 • fax: (952) 838-0199
e-mail: bullying411@pacer.org • website: www.pacer.org/bullying

Funded by the US Department of Education's Office of Special Education Programs, the National Center for Bullying Prevention is an advocate for children with disabilities and all children subject to bullying, from elementary through high school. Bullying and cyberbullying prevention resources (available in English, Spanish, Hmong, and Somali) include audiovideo clips, reading lists, creative writing exercises, group activities, and numerous downloadable handouts, such as "Bullying Fast Facts." The center sponsors school and community workshops and events such as National Bullying Awareness Week each October.

National Crime Prevention Council (NCPC)
2001 Jefferson Davis Hwy., Ste. 901, Arlington, VA 22202
(202) 466-6272 • fax: (202) 296-1356
website: www.ncpc.org/cyberbullying

The NCPC was founded in 1979 to get citizens, especially youth, involved in crime prevention. It is best known for televised public service announcements and school-based programs featuring McGruff the Crime Dog. Other novel approaches to addressing social problems include its Community Responses to Drug Abuse and Youth Outreach for Victim Assistance programs. The council's cyberbullying campaign includes a public service ad contest (winning ads are viewable on the website), free antibullying banners users can copy and paste into e-mail or social networking pages, the Be Safe and Sound in School program, and educational training manuals for youth and adults to manage bullying and intimidation. Downloadable resources include a range of podcasts and research papers, such as the Harris Interactive report *Teens and Cyberbullying*.

Olweus Bullying Prevention Program

Institute on Family and Neighborhood Life, Clemson University
158 Pool Agricultural Center, Clemson, SC 29634-0132
toll-free: (864) 710-4562 • fax: (406) 862-8971
e-mail: nobully@clemson.edu • website: www.clemson.edu/olweus

Developed by Norwegian bullying researcher Dan Olweus in the 1980s, this program is a school-based intervention program designed to prevent or reduce bullying in elementary, middle, and junior high schools (students six to fifteen years old). It is endorsed as a model antibullying program by the US Substance Abuse and Mental Health Services Administration and by the Office of Juvenile Justice and Delinquency Prevention. How the program works, statistical outcomes, and studies of the effectiveness of this and other antibullying programs are available on its website.

Wired Safety

1 Bridge St., Irvington-on-Hudson, NY 10533
(201) 463-88663 • fax: (201) 670-7002
e-mail: parry@aftab.com • website: www.wiredsafety.org

Wired Safety is an Internet safety and help group that offers articles, activities, and advice designed for seven- to seventeen-year-olds on a range of issues, including cyberbullying, cyberstalking, and cyberharassment. Resources include a Cyber 911 Help Line, a cyberstalking poll, cyberbullying Q&As, and a speakers bureau. Information available on the website covers Facebook privacy protections, how to handle sexting, building safe websites, and many other topics. Wired Safety also sponsors the annual Wired Kids Summer on Capitol Hill: In a role reversal, tech-savvy teens get the chance to present cybersafety research, raise cyberbullying issues, and tell industry and government leaders what they need to know about cybersafety.

Books

Sheri Bauman, *Cyberbullying: What Counselors Need to Know.* Alexandria, VA: American Counseling Association, 2010.

Barbara Coloroso, *The Bully, the Bullies, and the Bystander: From Preschool to High School; How Parents and Teachers Can Help Break the Cycle of Violence.* New York: HarperCollins Living, 2008.

Edward F. Dragan, *The Bully Action Guide: How to Help Your Child and Get Your School to Listen.* New York: Palgrave Macmillan, 2011.

Susan Eikov Green, *Don't Pick on Me: Help for Kids to Stand Up to and Deal with Bullies.* Oakland, CA: Instant Help, 2010.

Sameer Hinduja and Justin W. Patchin, *Bullying Beyond the Schoolyard: Preventing and Responding to Cyberbullying.* Thousand Oaks, CA: Corwin, 2008.

Tom Jacobs, *Teen Cyberbullying Investigated: Where Do Your Rights End and Consequences Begin?* Minneapolis: Free Spirit, 2010.

Meline Kevorkian and Robin D'Antona, *101 Facts About Bullying: What Everyone Should Know.* Lanham, MD: Rowman and Littlefield, 2008.

Robyn MacEachern, *Cyberbullying: Deal with It and Ctl Alt Delete It.* Toronto: J. Lorimer, 2008.

Samuel C. McQuade III, James B. Colt, and Nancy Meyer, *Cyber Bullying: Protecting Kids and Adults from Online Bullies.* Westport, CT: Praeger, 2009.

Alexis A. Moore, *A Parents' Guide to Cyberstalking and Cyberbullying.* El Dorado Hills, CA: Survivors in Action, 2010.

Shaheen Shariff, *Confronting Cyber-bullying: What Schools Need to Know to Control Misconduct and Avoid Legal Consequences.* Cambridge: Cambridge University Press, 2008.

Shaheen Shariff and Andrew H. Churchill, *Truths and Myths of Cyber-bullying: International Perspectives on Stakeholder Responsibility and Children's Safety*. New York: Peter Lang, 2010.

Periodicals and Internet Sources

Nick Abrahams and Victoria Dunn, "Is Cyber-bullying a Crime?," *Sydney Morning Herald* (Australia), May 21, 2009.

Adweek, "Bully Pulpit: Agencies Tackle the Problem of Cyberbullying with Teen-Targeted Campaigns That Aim to Silence the Crescendo of Abuse," October 25, 2010.

Timothy Birdnow, "Cyberbullying Laws and the Moral Code," *American Thinker*, May 24, 2009.

Tony Bradley, "What Are Your Kids Doing Online?," *PC World*, June 2011.

Michelle Catalano, "Cyberbullying: Despicable, but Criminal?," *Pajamas Media*, May 22, 2008. www.pajamasmedia.com.

Elizabeth Charnock, "How to Prevent Cyberbullying? Monitor," *San Francisco Chronicle*, September 2, 2009.

Lauren Collins, "Friend Game: Behind the Online Hoax That Led to a Girl's Suicide," *New Yorker*, January 21, 2008.

William Creeley, "Why the Tyler Clementi Act Threatens Free Speech on Campuses," *Chronicle of Higher Education*, April 10, 2011.

Michelle R. Davis, "Schools Tackle Legal Twists and Turns of Cyberbullying," *Digital Directions*, February 9, 2011.

Maureen Dowd, "Stung by the Perfect Sting," *New York Times*, August 26, 2009.

Economist, "Megan's Law: Cyber-bullying and the Courts," July 11, 2009.

Karen Fanning, "Cyberspace Bullies: Why Do So Many Kids Turn to Cyberbullying? How Can You Help Stop It?," *Junior Scholastic*, November 9, 2009.

Megan Feldman, "Why Are Nice, Normal Girls Getting Bullied Online?," *Glamour*, March 2010.

Susan Hayes, "Cyberbullies R 4 Real: Bullies Have a New Strategy for the 21st Century," *Current Health 2*, April 1, 2008.

Janet Kornblum, "Cyberbullying Grows Bigger and Meaner," *USA Today*, July 15, 2008.

Robin M. Kowalski, "Cyber Bullying," *Psychiatric Times*, October 1, 2008.

Amanda Lenhart, "Teens and Sexting," Pew Internet & American Life Project, December 15, 2009. www.pewinternet.org.

Judith Levine, "What's the Matter with Teen Sexting?," *American Prospect*, February 2, 2009.

Lynda Lopez, "How a Cyberbully Almost Ruined My Life," *New York Times Upfront*, September 6, 2010.

Los Angeles Times, "Overreaction to Online Harassment," August 22, 2009.

Damon Poeter, "Study: A Quarter of Parents Say Their Child Involved in Cyberbullying," *PC Magazine*, July 14, 2011.

Helen A.S. Popkin, "Cyberbullying Laws Won't Save Your Children," MSNBC, May 15, 2009. www.msnbc.com.

Neil J. Rubenking, "Monitor Your Child's Every Move Online," *PC Magazine*, July 2011.

Jonathan Turley, "Bullying's Day in Court," *USA Today*, July 15, 2008.

University of Arizona Daily Wildcat, "Freedom of Speech Preempts 'Cyberbullying' Rules," July 25, 2009.

Jimmy Wales and Andrea Weckerle, "Keep a Civil Cybertongue," *Wall Street Journal*, December 29, 2009.

Kathy Wilmore, "Cyberbullying: Technology Is Making Bullying Easier to Do, and Harder to Escape," *Junior Scholastic*, November 22, 2010.

Saray Zay, "What Sticks and Stones Can't Do, Facebook Will— and More!," *USA Today* (magazine), March 2011.

INDEX

A

Adolescent Web Awareness Requires Education Act (AWARE Act, proposed), 57, 62, 73

Adults
  as bullies, types of, 59
  bullying children online should be prosecuted, 57–63
  responsibility in preventing cyberbullying, 24–25

Ames, Champion v. (1903), 47

AWARE (Adolescent Web Awareness Requires Education) Act (proposed), 57, 62, 73

B

Barack, Lauren, 39
Bazelon, Emily, 76
Bell, Emily, 33–34
Blumenfeld, Warren, 6
Born Digital (Palfrey), 62
Brown, Asher, 5
Buder, Emily, 30–31
Buder, Sarah, 30–31

Bullying
  by adults, types of, 59
  cyberbullying is worse than, 32–38
  facts/myths about, *27*
  is not a rite of passage for youth, 23–31
  offline *vs.* online, prevalence of, *46*

percentage of youth victimized online also experiencing in person, 81
prevalence of, *19, 28, 50*
prevalence of students missing school to avoid, *15*

C

Campus gossip sites, 35–36
  universities' responses to, 38
Champion v. Ames (1903), 47
Chase, Raymond, 6
Chickering, Arthur, 36
Cintron, Rosa, 32, 33
Civil Rights Act (1964), 65
Clementi, Tyler, 5, 69
  vigil for, *7*
Communication Decency Act (1996), 62
Constitution, US. *See* First Amendment; Tenth Amendment
Cook, Sarah Gibbard, 32
Creeley, William, 64
Culberson, John, 73
Curry, Adrianne, 7
Cyberbullies, 44
  characteristics of, 13
  most are young, 47
Cyberbullying
  by adults of children, should be criminalized, 57–63
  consequences of, 13–14
  criminalization of, would be ineffective, 49–56